Quintcannon:

Line of Play

Ken Knee

Quintcannon:
Line of Play

Ken Knee

Copyright © 2016 by Ken Knee

ISBN 978-1-61529-171-7

Published by Vista Books Ltd.
1115 D Street
Ramona, CA 92065

Chapter 1

Murder is Not a Game

For the past six weeks Detective Lieutenant Kenne Quintcannon uses his day off exercising to try and get his body back into perfect physical condition after abusing it for ten years. At the age of thirty-five getting an abused body back to perfect physical condition is no small task because Kenne's job doesn't give him the time needed to accomplish it. But he keeps trying. Besides the physical exercise, he also exercises his frustrations, fantasies and humility to the limit. He does this by playing pick-up basketball games at the renowned Venice Beach courts where, from time to time, a cool Pacific Ocean breeze cools off the sweating participants on a hot summer day. But not today.

Two teams are embattled in a hotly contested, full court basketball game. One team is wearing T-shirts; the other team is bare-chested. Kenne, a member of the bare-chested or skins team, is dribbling the basketball toward the opponent's basket as fast as his aging and out-of-condition legs will carry him. As he nears the basket he leaps in the air with the ball extended in his right hand. At that instant he is clobbered by a large, younger opponent in a T-shirt who stands about six-foot seven-inches tall. He blocks Kenne's shot and is able to tip the ball to one of his teammates in the same motion. Kenne is knocked to the ground and the other opponent retrieves the loose ball and starts dribbling up the court.

Everyone except Kenne and the large man who leveled him, follow the dribbler up the court. He dunks the basketball when he gets to the basket on the opposite end of the court. Kenne remains lying on his back, not moving, while the large man is standing over him and looking down. The opponent grinds his teeth and growls at Kenne before he walks away without saying a word.

Kenne Narration: "Six weeks ago, before I started on this special conditioning program, I would not have been able to get up from that hit. Actually, I'm not sure that conditioning program is working. I think I'm going to need some help, here."

The players with their shirts on are celebrating with high fives as they walk off the court while the skins players still standing walk off, dejectedly. One of Kenne's teammates notices him still lying on his back at the opposite end of the court. He's a six-foot five-inch tall, muscle bound black man. He walks towards Kenne and peers down at him when he arrives.

Kenne Narration: "That's my best friend, Harley Guerrero. He's going to nag me about playing out of control. He knows me like a book. I've been playing that way ever since I was a teenager on the high school basketball team and I'm too old to change my game."

"You can get up now," Harley says in a sarcastic voice. "We lost."

"If I could get up, I would," Kenne informs him.

Harley shakes his head and then extends his right arm down toward Kenne. Kenne grabs the big right hand and Harley pulls him to his feet, which is no small task as Kenne carries two-hundred and twenty-five pounds on his six-foot three-inch frame. Slowly, they walk towards a park bench where their shirts are sitting.

"That was one hell of a drive, Kenne," Harley says sarcastically. "But don't you think a bit out of control."

Kenne Narration: "See. What did I tell you? I don't know why I put up with his nagging. I guess it's because we've been friends for so long."

"When are you going to learn that you can't do it yourself," Harley continues his nagging. "Basketball is a team game designed to involve all five players. You've got to keep the ball moving and hit the open man. You have to pay more attention to the fundamentals to get the maximum reward out of the game."

In a harsh tone of voice, Kenne replies, "Harley, please. This is not the NBA. It's playground basketball for Christ sake. Who cares?"

"I do," Harley answers him.

"That's because of your sports psychology degree. Everything in sports has to be perfect with you."

"What's wrong with that?"

Kenne doesn't answer him as the two men reach the park bench. Kenne opens a small cooler sitting on the bench and pulls out two bottles of cold water. He tosses one of them to Harley. Both men take a long swig of the cold water and then a deep breath. Kenne bends over and pours the rest of the water in his bottle over his head. Harley follows suit.

"Oh, that feels so good," Kenne says.

"Oh, yeah," Harley utters in a deep voice.

Kenne grabs a towel sitting on the bench and wipes off his head and face. He then hands the towel to Harley who does the same.

Harley picks up his t-shirt and puts it on. Kenne picks his t-shirt up and slings it over his shoulder. He also picks up his cell phone that was lying under his t-shirt and turns it on looking for messages. There isn't any.

"Now, that's a bad attitude," Harley scolds him. "You can't expect to perform at peak efficiency with an attitude like who cares."

"Peak efficiency?" Kenne says with a puzzled expression. "I'm not an automobile, Harley. I'm a human being. Now, let's just forget about it."

"And, another thing. That guy fouled you. Why didn't you call it? In fact, the bastard mugged you."

Kenne answers him calmly, "I thought the rules were no blood, no foul."

Kenne turns and walks toward the parking lot while putting his t-shirt on. Harley follows close behind.

"You never were a bleeder," Harley remarks.

"I can bleed as well as the next guy. It's just that I need a better reason than a basketball game," Kenne answers his remark.

"You know, you're impossible!" Harley says disgustedly.

"Yeah, I know. I like it that way," Kenne says with a smile. "And I've had just about enough of your sports psychology for one day. Either change the subject or take a bus ride home."

Harley has an aversion to riding the bus so he quickly changes the subject.

"I read in the paper where the Los Angeles County Sheriff's office has taken over the domino killing investigation. Who's in charge?"

"I am," Kenne answers.

The two men reach Kenne's unmarked police car. Kenne pulls his keys out from his right front pants pocket and uses the automatic door opener to unlock the doors. As he opens the driver's side front door, his cell phone rings.

Harley whistles and then says, "Wow!! That's quite a case. What's the count now, three victims?"

Kenne ignores Harley and answers his cell phone.

"This is Quintcannon."

Kenne listens to a voice on the other end for about fifteen seconds. While the voice is talking he turns his back to Harley and leans against the side of his unmarked squad car.

"I'm about twenty minutes away," Kenne informs the voice on the other end of his cell phone.

Kenne closes the cell phone and shoves it into his left front pants pocket and turns toward Harley.

"As of this afternoon, four," Kenne answers Harley's earlier question.

Kenne gets into his car in a rush. Harley does the same on the passenger side. Kenne starts the car and then reaches toward the dashboard and turns on the siren and flashing blue and yellow lights on the roof. Both he and Harley fasten their seat belts and Kenne backs out of the parking space and drives off at a very fast pace. The lights on the roof are swirling and the siren screaming.

Kenne's car is traveling at a high rate of speed through the streets of west L.A. Cars traveling in both directions move toward the curb to make way for him.

Kenne Narration: "When I asked Harley to change the subject, he sure picked a dandy. Let me bring you up to speed on the domino killings. For the past three months or so we've had a serial killer active in Los Angeles County. We've dubbed him the domino killer because he has placed a domino in the right hand of each of his victims, and it appears that he's struck again."

****

A large number of police officers are standing around as Kenne arrives at the crime scene. Kenne gets out of his car and

Detective Lamar Cole, a member of Kenne's Detective Squad greets him. Cole, a young black man, that is as tall as Kenne but much thinner has been in the Los Angeles County Sheriff's detective unit a little more than two years. He is aggressive and eager to learn. As usual he is wearing a suit, tie, and plain white shirt. His black shoes have a high shine to them.

"Sorry to bother you on your day off," Lamar says apologetically.

Kenne smiles at him and sarcastically states, "Of course you are," then Kenne removes the smile and sternly says, "Talk to me."

"We've got Domino's victim number four in the alley," Lamar informs Kenne.

Kenne walks toward the victim lying in the alley under a coroner's blanket. Lamar walks alongside him.

Lamar continues, "A domino was in his right hand, just like the other three. The coroner says he probably died instantly from a blow to the head. He'll know more after he performs an autopsy."

"Any I.D. on him?" Kenne asks.

"It's just like the others. No I.D. No wallet. But we've got a witness who can identify him. Sort of."

Kenne stops walking, looks at Lamar and quizzically asks, "Sort of?"

"Yeah. She saw something but she's not sure if she can identify the perpetrator."

"Perpetrator?"

"Yeah, perpetrator. You know, the doer. The guy that did it." Lamar pauses a few seconds, than continues, "The killer, Lieutenant."

"You mean the alleged killer," Kenne corrects him.

"Yes, the alleged killer," Lamar agrees. "Or, the alleged perpetrator."

Kenne nods his head a few times and grins at Lamar.

"Where is this witness?" Kenne asks.

Lamar points to a very pretty, young light-skinned black woman standing near two uniform policemen about fifty feet from the body. Kenne turns and looks at the woman for a few moments and notices that she stands about five-foot five-inches, weighs around one-hundred-twenty pounds and is well dressed. He walks toward her. Lamar follows him.

"Who is she?" Kenne asks.

Her name is Alicia Jackson, and I've got all her information in here," Lamar answers waving his notebook, enthusiastically. "I've got her address, home and cell phone numbers, email address and she told me the time of the assault. It occurred about one o'clock. One 'O six to be exact."

"What about her birth date, occupation, recreational activities and what she had for breakfast this morning?" Kenne asks in a serious tone of voice.

"I've never had to get that kind of information before," Lamar says in a concerned tone. "Is that information important?"

"It's not." Kenne laughs. "I'm just getting even for your continued use of that perpetrator word."

Kenne walks up to Alicia Jackson. Lamar follows him and stands close by.

"Miss Jackson, I'm Detective Lieutenant Quintcannon with the Los Angeles County Sheriff's Department," Kenne greets her. "I'm in charge of this investigation"

Alicia extends her right hand and Kenne shakes it, gently.

"Nice to meet you," Alisha says with a quizzical look on her face as she observes Kenne's unusual attire.

His t-shirt is soaking wet from sweat and his hair is messy from being wiped with the towel.

"Excuse the appearance," Kenne pleads. "Today's my day off and I've been working out."

Alicia nods her head and quips, "Actually, I think it's very fashionable. You could probably qualify as a poster boy for GQ."

Lamar laughs and Kenne gives him an evil glance. Lamar turns away and stops laughing.

"Laughing Detective Cole over there tells me you know the victim," Kenne says getting down to the business at hand.

Lisa answers in a stressful voice, "Not really. I mean, I've seen him around the neighborhood, but I don't know his name. I think he lives nearby. But I'm really not sure."

"Did you see the perpetrator?" Kenne asks in a loud enough voice so Detective Cole can hear him.

Detective Cole looks down at the ground and smiles.

"Only briefly," she answers. "He was running away."

"Tell me what you can about him? Approximate height, weight, did he have a limp? Whatever you can."

"It's kind of hard to tell. He was so far away."

"Take your time and think back," Kenne says, patiently.

Alicia turns and looks down the alley for a moment. She turns back and looks at Kenne.

"I'd say he was a small man and a little on the thin side," Alicia decides. "Maybe my height. Not much taller."

Alicia pauses for a moment and then continues, "I really can't be sure. It happened so fast."

"That's okay, you're doing fine," Kenne encourages her. "What was he wearing?"

"All black. I'm sure of that. Black pants and sweat shirt. The kind with a hood. The hood was pulled up over his head."

"How about gloves? Was he wearing gloves?"

"Maybe. I can't be sure."

"By any chance did you happen to get a look at his face?"

"No. His back was toward me."

"Where do you work?"

"At Jack's Furniture Outlet on Wilshire near Vermont."

"What do you do there?"

"I'm a sales associate."

"What were you doing here at one o'clock. Shouldn't you be at work?"

"I took a personal day off. Doctor's appointment. I was on my way home from that."

Kenne turns towards Lamar who is writing down all the information in his little notebook.

Did you get it all, detective?" Kenne asks Lamar.

"Yes sir. I've got it all," Lamar snaps back.

"Detective Cole, do me a favor and get a business card for Ms. Jackson out of my glove box."

Lamar sticks his notebook and pen in his inside jacket pocket and walks off towards Kenne's car. Kenne turns and faces Alicia.

"If you think of anything else, I'd appreciate a call," Kenne addresses her.

"I'll do that."

Kenne turns his attention toward the two Sheriff's Department uniform officers standing close by.

"Which one of you two men suggested we canvas the neighborhood for someone who can identify the victim?" Kenne asks them.

The two officers look at each other with puzzled looks on their faces.

"I think it's a great idea," Kenne informs them.

"We'll get right on it, Lieutenant," Officer Martinez says with enthusiasm.

"You might also ask around if anyone saw our serial killer," Kenne continues to give instructions to the two officers. "A guy dressed in black with a hood over his head."

"Yes sir. That's a good idea, too," Officer Goodman responds.

The two officers hurry off as Detective Cole returns with one of Kenne's business cards for Ms. Jackson. He hands the business card to her. She looks at it and then walks away. Kenne and Cole watch her as she disappears into the on looking crowd of people.

"Assemble the whole detective squad for a meeting in one hour in the squad room," Kenne instructs Lamar. "Also, inform the coroner that I want his report as soon as possible. And, have him run prints on the deceased. Maybe we'll get lucky and he'll have a record."

Kenne walks toward his patrol car where Harley is leaning against the right front door of the car.

"You still want a ride?" Kenne asks Harley in a surly voice.

"The way you drive," Harley jokes.

Kenne gets into his car. Harley joins him. Kenne starts the car and looks at Harley with an evil eye.

Harley smiles at Kenne and informs him, "I'm not walking."

Kenne drives away from the crime scene, slowly.

****

Harley notices that Kenne's mind seems to be in another world as he follows traffic.

"That domino killer has really put you in an ugly mood," Harley says to break the silence.

Kenne takes his eyes off the road, glances at Harley and responds, "Murder puts me in an ugly mood."

"This domino fellow has you in a quandary."

"Quandary. That's a good word. It fits. I know four things about him. He leaves a domino with each victim so he can get credit for the murder. He probably wants us to refer to him as the domino killer or maybe just Domino. His victims have absolutely nothing in common. And, the domino left with each victim is loaded with clues about where he's going to strike again. The problem with the clues is they are too vague. We can't figure them out and they lead nowhere until he strikes again."

"Maybe Domino is his real name," Harley surmises.

"I'm afraid not. We checked the name out from every angle and came up with a blank."

"He might be playing a game."

"A game?" Kenne questions Harley.

"Yeah. A game of dominoes."

Kenne stops for a red light and looks at Harley.

"What are you talking about?" Kenne asks.

Harley answers Kenne's question with one of his own.

"Do you know anything about dominoes?"

"Sure. I know a lot," Kenne answers.

"Tell me what you know."

"Dominoes are rectangular tiles with dots on them, similar to dice. They're usually black with white dots but they also come in white with black dots."

Kenne pauses and passes a fleeting glance at Harley. He is laughing silently to himself.

"That's it?" Harley asks Kenne.

"No. I've heard that people stand them on end in long lines so when the first one is toppled, it topples all of the tiles," Kenne answers and then nods his head.

Harley laughs again and then informs Kenne, "Those dots are called pips. And, there are actual rules to the game of dominoes," Harley informs Kenne. "In fact, there are a number of variations to the game."

"How do you know that?" Kenne asks in the same annoyed voice.

"My dad was a dominoes champion when he was in college. When I was a kid, he would insist on playing at least one game of dominoes with me every night before bedtime. He used to tell me playing dominoes helps build character and a sharp mind."

Both men sit silent while Kenne pays attention to his driving.

Harley continues, "The lining up of dominoes so they can topple is not a game of dominoes. Actually, the phenomenon of small events causing similar effects that leads to eventual catastrophe is called the domino effect. It has nothing to do with the game of dominoes."

"What the hell was that all about?" Kenne asks.

"Never mind."

"Since you know so much about dominoes and the game has given you such a sharp mind, how about sitting in on my squad meeting," Kenne asks.

"Okay. But take me home first. I need to clean up."

"So do I, but we don't have enough time. We can shower and change clothes in the locker room at headquarters."

"I don't have a change of clothes with me," Harley says.

"I've got a change for both of us in my locker."

Harley smiles at Kenne and asks him, "Does this mean I can bill the department for my time?"

Kenne ignores the question.

****

Lieutenant Quintcannon and his homicide detective squad work out of the second floor of the West Los Angeles Branch of the Los Angeles County Sheriff's Department. It's a four story building made out of steel and concrete. The roof is flat with a thick steel reinforcement because it is home to a heliport. The east wall of the squad room is lined with file cabinets. The west wall has three large windows. Kenne is standing at the center window, staring out into the evening sunset. He is wearing black dress slacks and an orange sport shirt that blends in with the distant sunset.

Detective Cole walks up behind Kenne and informs him, "Everyone's here, Lieutenant."

"It's beautiful, isn't it," Kenne says as if in a trance.

"Beautiful?" Lamar says in bewilderment.

"The sunset." Kenne pauses then profoundly states, "It's the last beautiful thing on Earth."

Kenne turns and walks away, stating, "Let's get started."

Kenne walks past a cork bulletin board sitting on an easel and stops in front of a rectangular folding table near the easel. Lamar follows him and sits down in a chair facing the front. There are seven detectives in Kenne's squad, including Lamar. The room is filled with eight desks in three rows. The front and middle row have three desks each with the back row having two desks.

Detective Sam Hartenstein occupies the desk on the far right in the first row near the windows. Sam is 51-years old and has been a detective with the Sheriff's Department for sixteen years. He is the nearest thing the squad has to a computer aficionado. Whenever the squad needs information on a case, Sam uses the internet to the maximum of his abilities.

Sam is married with three children but only one is still living at home. He wears black horned-rim glasses. He is five-foot ten-inches tall with a slight build. He weighs about one-hundred-seventy-five pounds. He has a thick mustache that's turning gray along with his hair and he keeps both well groomed. He's wearing a long-sleeve button-down light blue sport shirt and his sport jacket is hanging from the back of his chair. He is sitting at his desk, hands folded in front of him, waiting for the meeting to start.

Detective Joshua Bradley is sitting on the front edge of the middle desk in the front row. He is facing Kenne. This desk is his home base when he isn't working undercover for the squad. Joshua is thirty-one years old and stands six-foot two-inches tall and weighs in the neighborhood of two-hundred pounds. He's single and lives with his Asian girlfriend in Alhambra, a long trek from the office. He is dressed in a soiled t-shirt, faded blue jeans and scruffy sneakers and he has a three-day growth on his face. Josh has been with the squad a little over a year. He was transferred from the County Sheriff's East Los Angeles office to take the place of retired Detective J. J. Fitzpatrick. (The J. J. stands for John Joseph.)

The desk in the front row to Kenne's left is occupied by Detective Terri McDonald. Terri is the only female member of the squad and besides Kenne the only one with a Masters Degree in Forensics. She is sitting at her desk and as usual is immaculately dressed in a brown suit and fancy lace blouse. Terri is a smallish, 28-year old single woman and an expert in the martial arts. In fact, she takes pride in her athleticism. She has been a member of Kenne's squad for three years.

Kenne hung Terri with the nickname 'Mac' the first day she reported to work. Terri hates the nickname and that's probably why the whole squad has picked up on it. Actually, she should be flattered because she is the only member of the squad that Kenne has laid a nickname on at first site. Her latest assignment has been working closely with him and Lamar on the domino slayings.

Detective Alfonso Ramirez works at the first desk in the second row near the windows. He's been a member of Kenne's squad a little more than four years. Although Ramirez, who is 34-years old, is of Spanish descent he speaks and understands four languages; English, Spanish, French and German. He has a muscular body on his six-foot frame. He is a flashy dresser always wearing bright colors. Today is no different as he is wearing a bright purple sport shirt. He is sitting on the right front edge of his desk.

The middle desk in the second row is vacant because Kenne has set it up as a memorial to slain Detective Sergeant Trevor Russell. Russell was killed eighteen months ago during a fire fight with bank robbers. The bank robbers were apprehended and put away for thirty-five years. Detective Sergeant Russell was put away for eternity and Kenne has trouble forgetting it. Kenne and Trevor were roommates at UCLA for two years and attended the Police Academy together.

The desk to the right of the memorial is manned by Detective Anthony Tropazinni. Trop, as he is known to everyone is of full-blooded Italian heritage and speaks fluent Italian. He is five-foot ten-inches tall and weighs one-hundred-eighty pounds. He is 53-years old and divorced for three years. Trop has been a detective with the Sheriff's Department for twenty-four years. He is strongly considering retiring in a year or so with a twenty-five year pension. He is a seasoned veteran and Kenne would hate to lose him. Ever efficient, he is filling out an arrest report while he waits for the meeting to start.

The two desks in the back row belong to Detective Cole and Detective Sergeant Dave Singleton. Singleton is second in command of the squad and Kenne's right hand man. He is 46-years old and a member of the Sheriff's Department for twenty-two years. He is small in stature compared to the other male members of the squad. He carries about one-hundred-fifty pounds on his small frame. He is dressed in a brown suit with a red bow tie that stands out against his white shirt. He is sitting to Kenne's right near the bulletin board.

Harley is sitting at the end of the table to Kenne's left. Harley is wearing one of Kenne's pullover sport shirts. It is too small and looks as if it was form fitted to his upper body. The pair of pants he has borrowed from Kenne is short and ends just above his ankles. On the table in front of Harley are four black domino pieces.

Kenne looks around the room and notices the concerned looks on everyone's face. He looks everyone in the eye then starts pacing back and forth in front of the table his right hand rubbing his forehead. He stops pacing and turns, facing the squad members.

"We're in a lot of trouble, here," he says in a loud voice startling everyone. "We've got a maniac filling our streets with dead bodies and the media is clamoring for our necks. They want to know why we haven't come up with any leads on this … this maniac. And that's only the beginning. The powers that be upstairs want answers to their questions, and they've got plenty of them. And I want some answers, too. Our necks are all the way out to Pomona so we're going to put our heads together and get some positive results on finding this maniac and I don't care how long it takes. From this moment on every one of you will be spending every waking hour working on this case. I've decided to give this serial killer a name. Domino."

Harley looks at Kenne with a puzzled look on his face. He has never seen this side of his personality.

Kenne starts pacing again and addresses the squad while doing so.

"We've missed a lot so we're going to start from the beginning and cover all the bases. Before we do, I believe all of you have noticed that large handsome man with the form fitting shirt and short pants sitting at the table. His name is Harley Guerrero and he is a dominoes expert. Or so he claims."

Harley nods his head and smiles.

"Mr. Guerrero has volunteered his services in trying to understand what the domino killer is trying to tell us," Kenne continues.

Harley shakes his head in amazement as Kenne turns, looks at him and winks. Kenne picks up a pointer sitting on the table and walks over to the bulletin board. He points the instrument at the upper right corner of the bulletin board where a coroner's picture of victim number one is pinned up. The victims name and other information appear below the picture.

Kenne starts in a normal voice, "Victim number one, Gilbert Patterson, a High School Principal without an enemy in the world, except for maybe a few truants. He was a small, gentle man but died violently. At a little after ten o'clock in the evening of April 17th, on a quiet residential street in North Hollywood, Gilbert took his dog for his nightly constitution. About twenty minutes later Gilbert was stabbed through the heart with - of all things - a railroad spike. According to the coroner, death was instantaneous. We believe the attacker knew this yet he proceeded to drive the railroad spike through Gilbert's body and into the ground beneath him with what we presume was a large hammer."

Kenne points to the railroad spike lying on right side of the table.

"Then he also took the time to rummage through Gilbert's pockets looking for a wallet and he also placed a domino in Gilbert's right hand."

Kenne pauses for a moment and Harley stands up and slides the domino that was placed in Gilbert's right hand to the center of the table. It has five white pips on one square end and three white pips on the other end. He lays the domino with the three pips facing to his left.

Kenne continues, "The attacker left no finger prints on the railroad spike or anything else in the vicinity. There were no eye witnesses and Sam has searched the internet for hours trying to find a precedent. Sam found out that committing murder with a railroad spike isn't an everyday occurrence. So far he's come up with nothing. However, Sam's internet investigation came up with some interesting current facts about railroad spikes. Tell us about it, Sam."

Sam opens a notebook that's sitting on his desk. He thumbs through the pages until he gets to the page he wants. He glances at the information he has written down and clears his throat.

"Well, Lieutenant, it seems that railroad spikes are just as popular today as they were in the Wild, Wild West when track was being laid for what is now our coast to coast rail system."

"Enough with the history lesson, Sam," Kenne interrupts. "Get to the point."

Sam clears his throat again and continues, "Much to my surprise they are still manufacturing railroad spikes. A company in Pennsylvania is the largest producer. I took it upon myself to call the company. I talked to their sales manager, a Mr. Bill Bartholomew. We had quite a chat. He told me that the only customers in the Los Angeles area that buy railroad spikes or any other railroad supplies are movie studios. But none of them have bought anything in the last three years."

"And what did you do with this information?" Kenne asks.

"Trop and I called all of the movie studios and came up with very little. It seems that when most of the studios are finished with movie props they sell them to collectors. It avoids storage expenses. That's what happened to most of the railroad spikes. However, two studios frown upon selling or auctioning their movie props. We ran into a dead end there. They checked their inventory and nothing is missing."

"How about the collectors who buy that kind of stuff? Did you get names?" Kenne enthusiastically asks.

"Yeah, we did. There are three local collectors and we checked them out. One is a Philanthropist, another is a heart surgeon and the third one is a member of the Los Angeles City Council. I'm afraid another dead end, Lieutenant."

"Then we still have to assume Domino might be a railroad yard worker or the like," Kenne states. "Let's move on to victim number two."

Kenne points at a picture of victim number two pinned to the bulletin board."

"Eric Van Horn, a fifty-five year old truck driver, had just locked up his delivery truck for the weekend behind his place of employment in East Los Angeles. He turned around into an eight-inch knife blade being thrust into his heart. According to the coroner he was stabbed eight times in the heart. The knife was left in Van Horn's heart after the eighth thrust."

Kenne points to the knife lying next to the railroad spike on the table.

"The attack occurred on Friday, May third, at about three o'clock in the afternoon, miles away from Domino's first attack. Once again no finger prints or clues left by the attacker. And, Gilbert and Eric have absolutely nothing in common."

Kenne turns and points at the domino on the table with the eight pips.

"Our serial killer left this domino in Eric's right hand to clue us when his next attack was going to occur. At least that's what we've assumed. May third is five-three. Reverse the numbers and you get three five. The coroner puts the time of death around three o'clock in the afternoon. Maybe at three 'O five. Three, five. And finally, five plus three equals eight. Mr. Van Horn was stabbed eight times. Patterson was killed on the seventeenth. One plus seven equals eight. The number eight also appears in the size of the weapon. A knife with an eight-inch blade. The number eight seems to be an important number regarding this attack. The only thing he didn't clue us in with the first domino killing was where he was going to strike again."

Detective Bradley whistles and then says, "Eight inches. That's one BAD ASS knife."

"Yes it is," Kenne acknowledges. "And it gets worse."

Kenne turns and looks at Detective MacDonald and asks her, "Mac, what can you tell us about this bad ass knife?"

"It's illegal to carry that size knife around. In fact, anything over three inches is illegal in California."

"Do you think Domino cares whether his murder weapons are illegal?" Kenne asks.

"Of course not. The thing is the law is contradictory. Although it's illegal to carry a knife over three inches long, you can buy any size illegal knife at any retail outlet or pawn shop without any questions asked."

"You're a forensics expert," Kenne states. "Is there any chance of let's say maybe one in a thousand of locating where this knife came from?"

"More like one in ten or twenty thousand," she states as a matter of fact.

Kenne puts his right hand to his jaw and rubs it for a few seconds before picking up the second domino.

"This domino was placed in Mr. Van Horn's right hand," Kenne says. "It has three pips on one side and one pip on the other. If the last clue gave us a date and approximate time of Domino's next attack, this one made some sort of sense because on May 25th he struck again. Only this time his favorite number was four.

"On that day at around four in the morning he attacked and killed homeless person, Willie Jackson, in downtown L.A. using an ice pick. He stabbed him four times. The coroner's report identifies the ice pick at four inches long."

The ice pick is sitting on the table next to the railroad spike and knife. Willie's picture, taken by the coroner is pinned on the bulletin board next to Van Horn's picture.

Kenne sets the domino tile down on the table and continues, "May 25th is three weeks and one day from Mr. Van Horn's demise. That's three-one which totals four, also the time of Jackson's death with a four inch object."

Kenne sighs, shakes his head and continues. "There are no coincidences here. This psychopath knows exactly what he's doing. He's probably laughing at us right now. Getting back to victim number three, poor homeless Willie Jackson had a domino in his right hand."

Kenne points to the domino lying on the table. Its two sides show one pip and six pips.

Harley stands up and interrupts Kenne, "Let me explain something here."

Kenne turns toward Harley and smiles at him as he says, "Our dominoes expert has something to say. Go ahead."

Harley slides the domino with the one-three pip combination next to the first domino. He places the side with three pips next to the three pips on the first domino with the side with one pip facing towards the group.

Harley states, "The game of dominos isn't simple. Actually, there are a number of games that can be played but I'll make this real quick. When playing the game you have a number of tiles in your possession, usually seven to start, similar to a game of cards. The object is to place one of your tiles next to an open end or side of the tile matching the number of pips, like I've done here matching the threes. This is called a 'Line of Play'."

"How many tiles are there in a set of dominoes," Detective Ramirez asks.

"A traditional Sino-European domino set consists of twenty-eight pieces. A set of twenty-eight tiles is known as Double Six. And, a Double Nine set consists of fifty-five tiles," Harley answers.

Ramirez continues with another question, "Is this maniac going to give us twenty-eight victims?"

Harley shrugs his shoulders and says, "Could be, or maybe fifty-five."

Everybody shakes their head with blank stares on their faces. Trop rolls his eyes.

Kenne interrupts and continues with his dissection of the case and as he does so Harley connects the third domino that was left in Willie Jackson's hand with the one sides touching. The six pip side is facing toward the group.

"The Jackson domino pips total seven. Using logic from the first two dominoes, we theorized the following. Domino's next assault was going to take place on June 1st, six-one. Or six weeks and one day from the Jackson murder. Or, even still, one week and six days later, which would be June seventh. Three days ago. And, his assault would take place at either one or six o'clock, a.m. or p.m. Confusing isn't it. That's exactly what Domino's plan is. To confuse us as much as possible."

Kenne pauses a moment and then continues, "However, we now know all that logic is trashed because he struck again, today, June tenth, sixteen days later. Just as before the victim had a domino in his right hand. The pips on the domino are six and four."

The six-four domino is on the table in front of Harley. He slides the domino toward the 'Line of Play' and places the side with six pips to the left of the pile.

Detective McDonald declares, "He's playing a game with us and so far he's winning."

"Murder is not a game," Kenne shouts.

Chapter 2

Copy Cat

The next morning Kenne is sitting at the desk in his office. He is writing different scenarios for the six-four domino on a notepad. Detective Cole interrupts him as he enters the office.

Kenne looks up and asks Cole, "Well, have you got the forensic report on our latest victim?"

"Yep. I've got it right here," Cole says waving the report above his head. "And, I got a picture of the victim from the coroner and I pinned it to the bulletin board."

"Thank you. Now, tell me about the forensics report," Kenne quips.

Cole sits down in a chair near Kenne's desk and starts shuffling the papers on his lap. He picks up one of the pages and reads from it.

"The victim's time of death was approximately one p.m. on June tenth. The cause of death occurred from a bludgeoning to the head with a blunt instrument. He was administered seven blows to different parts of the head as if the blunt instrument struck him in a swinging motion."

"I've already figured that out," Kenne informs Cole. "What about his identity?"

"That information is here, too," Cole discloses as he shuffles through the paperwork again and pulls out another page. "Forensics ran his prints and found nothing. However, after our meeting yesterday I went back to the scene of the crime and scrounged around a few dumpsters. Lo and behold I found a sawed-off baseball bat that was covered in blood. I immediately took it to Forensics and this is what they found."

Kenne looks at Cole in amazement as the detective reads from the forensic report.

"The blunt instrument that caused the death of John Doe is a sawed-off baseball bat...."

Kenne interrupts, "Sixteen inches long."

Cole looks up at Kenne, smiles and then continues reading, "Sixteen inches long. The instrument is covered with blood that matches the victim's DNA. The bat is a Mickey Mantle Louisville Slugger model. The bat has been sawed off from the knob up."

"A Mickey Mantle Louisville Slugger," Kenne repeats. "Do you know why Domino used that model?"

"I have no idea," Cole answers.

Kenne informs him, "The pips on the Jackson domino are one-six, which totals seven. Mickey Mantle's uniform number with the Yankees was seven. We've got one sick serial killer here. He's even got the memory of a Yankee Legend involved in his crime spree."

"How do you know this stuff?" Cole asks Kenne.

Kenne smiles at him and answers, "That's why I'm the Lieutenant."

****

A short time later Detective Ramirez sticks his head into Kenne's office and tells him, "Lieutenant, there's a Deputy Sheriff Goodman here to see you."

"Show him in," Kenne responds.

Officer Goodman enters Kenne's office and says, "Remember me."

"Of course," Kenne replies.

"Our canvassing of the neighborhood paid off," Goodman informs Kenne. "The victims name is George Harrison. It seems he lived alone about three blocks from the attack. His landlady identified the body ten minutes ago."

"Does she have any idea why Harrison was in that alley at that time of day?"

"I asked her about that. The only thing she could think of is that he was probably taking a short cut home."

"Not a short cut home, a short cut to eternity," Kenne quips.

Just as Officer Goodman leaves Kenne's office, Detective Sam Hartenstein walks in and beckons Kenne with a finger as he tells him, "You need to see something I found on the Internet."

Kenne rises from his chair and follows Hartenstein to his desk. Hartenstein sits down and Kenne hunches and peers over his left shoulder.

"I found this article in the Greenville, South Carolina News," Sam says. "It's a feature story from 1954."

The headline is **Serial Killer Strikes Again**.

The article reads as follows:

Once again, last night at approximately nine o'clock the serial killer that Police Chief Charles Porterfield has dubbed Domino struck again for the third time. Michael Tremont was stabbed through the heart with a railroad spike and died instantly. The attack occurred near Academy Street in downtown Greenville.

Chief Porterfield says, "We have no clues as to who Domino might be. All we know is that he is deranged and we will eventually apprehend him."

The Greenville Police Department has issued warnings for people to stay off the streets at night because Domino has committed all three murders after dark. In each case, Domino has used a different instrument. His first victim was bludgeoned to death with a baseball bat and the second victim stabbed a number of times with a large knife. All three victims had a domino placed in their right hand.

Kenne stops reading and asks Sam, "How did you find this?"

Sam looks up at Kenne and matter-of-factly says, "The one thing I hadn't done before. I typed in railroad spike murders on the internet and this popped up."

"Call the Greenville Police Department and get whatever information you can on their domino killer and give me a printout of that article," Kenne orders Sam. "We might have a copy cat, here."

"That article is almost sixty-years old, Lieutenant."

Kenne walks back to his office without responding to Sam.

****

It's early afternoon and Kenne is dozing in his chair when Captain Ray Manning enters his office, notices that Kenne is asleep and announces his entrance, "Siesta time in West L. A.?"

Ray Manning is the Captain of Detectives in the West L.A. office and

Kenne's boss. He's in his late fifties, wears wire-frame glasses and is clean shaven. He always wears a suit and tie and brown shoes with a shine. Ray is five-foot-nine inches tall and weighs in the neighborhood of one-hundred-eighty pounds.

Kenne opens his eyes and yawns. He stretches and says, "You look like you need a break, Ray. Pull up a chair and join me."

"Very funny," Manning snaps back and then gets to the point why he's paying Kenne a visit. "What's this I hear that this psychopath Domino, as you call him, is a copy cat?"

Kenne picks up the printout of the article Sam gave him and hands it to Ray.

"What's this?" Ray asks.

Kenne points to the sheet of paper and instructs Ray, "Read that."

Ray sits down in a chair near Kenne's desk and reads the article. He looks up at Kenne a couple of times while reading it with a puzzled look on his face.

"What the hell is this?" he shrieks. "If this is some kind of joke, it isn't funny."

"It's no joke," Kenne informs Ray. "That article is sixty-years old and they had a psychotic maniac running loose in Greenville where ever in God's Country that is South Carolina in 1954."

"You mean we really do have a copy cat here?"

"That's the way it looks unless some ninety-year old is continuing his crime spree in Los Angeles," Kenne says sarcastically.

"We need to check this out," Ray advises.

"Sam is working on it."

At that very moment, Sam walks into Kenne's office and sits down in a chair next to Ray. He nods at Ray and greets him, "Captain."

Kenne extends his left hand and asks Sam, "Well, what have you got?"

Sam smiles at Kenne and says, "Sit back and relax. Have I got a tale to tell. I took your suggestion and called the Greenville Police Department and talked to a detective named Michael Farrington. He didn't know much about their domino serial killer case but he referred me to a retired homicide detective. He's ninety-three years-old and living in a retirement home in Charlotte, North Carolina. His mind is as sharp as that knife lying out there on the table and he filled me in on what he remembers about the serial killer.

"It all started in the fall of fifty-three. Their serial killer murdered a man in October and then again in February of fifty-four. The railroad spike killing occurred in May of fifty-four and that was the last one in Greenville."

"The last murder or last railroad spike?" Manning asks.

"The last murder," Sam answers with a smile on his face. "Each time he left a domino in the victim's right hand."

"Didn't they realize the dominoes possibly left clues even if they were vague?" Kenne asks.

"They thought the killer left the dominoes so he would be given credit for the murders."

Kenne shakes his head, looks at Ray and says, "I guess we've come a long way in sixty years."

Sam continues, "Like I said the third homicide was the last in Greenville and Sullivan, that's the old man, closed the case as unsolved when the murders stopped. Now, here's where the story presses onward. Sullivan tells me in August of fifty-six, another Domino slaying occurred. This time in Atlanta, Georgia. And then, four more homicides occurred in the Atlanta area over the next year and a half. They all went unsolved at the time and once again, a domino was left in all of the victim's right hand.

"Sullivan reopened his case and contacted the Atlanta police when he heard about the first slaying. He worked with the Atlanta police department for almost two years until they finally found a link to the serial killer's identity.

"Albert Hill was raised in Greenville. He was a high school dropout but went to trade school and became a lathe operator. He was employed for six years by a Greenville furniture manufacturer. The owner of the company died and his heirs closed the firm. Albert Hill was out of a job. That happened shortly after the railroad spike murder."

"He moved to Atlanta," Ray interrupts.

"Exactly," Sam answers. "In August of fifty-four Albert Hill got a job as a lathe operator for an Atlanta furniture manufacturer. He became inactive for two years before continuing his killing spree."

"How did they decide that Albert Hill was the serial killer?" Kenne asks.

"A young Atlanta homicide detective came up with the brilliant idea of checking with local unions for any members moving from Greenville to Atlanta during the fifty-four time frame. It turns out that Albert Hill was a union member and the only one that came up on the list.

"The Atlanta homicide department obtained a warrant and raided Hill's residence. In the house they found a set of dominoes with eight dominoes missing. The missing dominoes were the ones he left with his victims. Hill was arrested, tried and convicted in Georgia of five counts of first degree murder. He was sentenced to death and executed in fifty-nine. No one claimed the body."

"Did you get the sequence of dominoes Hill left?"

"I asked Sullivan about that," Sam answers. "He had no idea and we can't trace them. Nobody seems to know what happened to them."

"Looks like we've got a copy cat killer in Los Angeles County," Ray states.

"Sam, trace this Albert Hill's life starting in Greenville," Kenne instructs. "Check if he had any relatives. A wife. Children. Brothers. Sisters. Girl Friends. Anything you can dig up on him."

"You think our Domino is a second generation relative?" Ray inquires.

Kenne looks Ray in the eye and responds, "Or a third. Maybe he's out to finish what Hill started."

Sam is still sitting in his chair when Kenne roars at him, "Why are you still sitting there?"

Chapter 3

Four-Six or Six-Four

It's a little after six in the evening and Kenne is driving home in his unmarked squad car. The numbers four and six keep passing through his mind along with all the possible clues Domino has left with that six-four domino. When Kenne left the office Sam was still on the internet hunting for information on Albert Hill. It was like he was a ghost. Sam wasn't having any luck on finding anybody that might be related to him. Sam even called the ninety-three year old Sullivan again to see if he could help. The old man couldn't help him.

Kenne's cell phone rings and he answers through his Bluetooth, "This is Quint-cannon."

"Lieutenant Quintcannon, this is Alicia Jackson," the voice on the other end says.

"Miss Jackson. How nice of you to call. Do you have some more information for me?"

"That's why I'm calling. I did some more thinking and I might have some important information for you," she informs him.

"Tell me about it," Kenne says.

"Not on the telephone."

"Why not?"

"What I have to tell you should be in private," she informs Kenne. "Do you still have my address?"

"I remember it from Detective Cole's notes."

"I'm on the second floor, front." She pauses a moment and then asks Kenne, "Do you like pepperoni?"

"Yeah, but only on pizza," he answers.

"That's good. I ordered one."

Alicia hangs up the phone.

Kenne hangs up his cell phone and starts thinking, "What has Alicia got up her sleeve that she wants to bribe me with a pepperoni pizza."

****

Alicia greets Kenne at the door. She is wearing a tight top that highlights her copious breasts with shorts and fuzzy pink slippers. She takes a hold of Kenne's right hand and guides him inside her apartment. She steps back and looks him over from head to foot while putting a hand to her chin. She has a quizzical look on her face.

Kenne looks at her with a frown and says, "What?"

"I'm trying to decide if I like you better all dressed up or with your workout clothes on," Alicia enlightens him. "Although, I think you look much sexier the first time we met. You know, with your hair messed up and all."

Alicia steps forward and they both look at each other in the eyes. She puts your arms around Kenne's neck, looks up at him and softly says, "The pizza has been delivered."

At six-foot three, Kenne is about eight inches taller than Alicia so he puts his hands on her butt, lifts her one-hundred-twenty pound body up and plants an incredible wet kiss on her lips. She responds back. After they release their lips from each other Kenne says, "How about we let the pizza get cold."

Alicia smiles and says, "Oh, my. You have a wonderful way with words."

****

Kenne rolls over in bed, opens one eye and notices Alicia has deserted him. At that instant she walks into her bedroom and announces, "Coffee is made."

Kenne asks, "What time is it?"

"Six-forty-five."

Kenne notices that Alicia is dressed and she has put on her makeup. He sits up in bed and tells Alicia, "I'll drive you to work."

"No thanks," she responds. "Public transportation is faster than the freeway. I left you some cold pizza for breakfast or if you wish we can save it for dinner."

Alicia turns and walks out of the room. Kenne rises and walks towards the bedroom doorway only to see Alicia leave the apartment. He scratches his head and shrugs his shoulders.

After they made love last night Kenne asked Alicia what else she had seen the day before. Not your usual small talk. Alicia told him she thought she saw the killer holding something in his hand as he fled the scene. Kenne informed her about the sawed-off baseball bat and she said it looked something like that.

Before Kenne returned to his home in West Los Angeles to shower, shave and change clothes, he grabbed a cup of Alicia's coffee. After just one sip he said to himself, "Why don't we have coffee like this in the squad room?"

It took about an hour of grooming and he was on his way to his office. During the drive the four-six and six-four numbers kept popping into his head again

Kenne Narration: "You're probably thinking, what's the matter with me, getting personally involved with a witness on a case I'm working on. Actually, she's not a witness because she can't identify Domino. All she saw was a shadow. And besides, it's been a long time since I got personally involved with a good looking babe like Alicia. Unfortunately, at the moment it's more important that I concentrate on this psychotic serial killer."

****

Kenne enters the squad room, walks past Sam's desk and motions with his head to follow him into his office. Kenne sits down on the corner of his desk and Sam walks in holding a sheet of paper.

Kenne asks Sam, "What have you got for me?"

Sam hands the sheet of paper to Kenne and he looks at it. The paper is blank. He turns it over and the other side is also blank.

"Is this supposed to be a joke," Kenne roars.

"No Lieutenant, it's no joke. Albert Hill is a blank. I found nothing we can use on this guy. The only thing I did find on Hill is that he was born in Winston-Salem, North Carolina on March ninth, 1927. His birth certificate states that his mother was unwed. I researched her and it came up that she had no other children. I researched Hill's past and came up empty except that he was a member of a Lathe Operators Union on the east coast. I couldn't find any marriage license with his name on it or any record of him fathering any children."

"That's why the empty sheet of paper?" Kenne asks.

"Yeah. I thought you'd get a kick out of it," Sam says with a smirk on his face.

Kenne crumbles the sheet of paper in his left hand, throws it on the floor.

"I'm in a nasty mood and I don't appreciate your sense of humor, today," Kenne says in a nasty voice.

"I'm sorry, Lieutenant," Sam responds. "I just thought a little levity might ease the tension around here."

Kenne nods his head in agreement and says, "You're right, Sam. Sorry I snapped at you. On your way out have Detectives Cole and McDonald step into my office."

Kenne is sitting behind his desk when Detectives Cole and McDonald enter his office.

"Close the door and take a seat," he instructs them.

Before he left the office last night Kenne asked Cole and McDonald to document all possible four-six scenarios they could think of, including like kind items from previous domino clues.

"Let's compare what we got," Kenne states.

All three open their notepads.

"Let's start with four-six," Kenne says. "Here's what I've got. Four-six means this maniac might strike again in four weeks and six days from the last attack at four o'clock, four-o-six, six o'clock, or six-o-four. That could be a.m. or p.m. Probably, p.m. Basically the same as previous scenarios."

Cole and McDonald concur that they have those items on their list.

Kenne continues, "Four-six could also mean four days at six o'clock or four days and six hours later."

"Or six hours earlier," McDonald adds.

Kenne nods his head a couple of times toward McDonald and continues, "Or something new like the four could be four times six or four times ten in days, minutes or hours."

"I don't have those items on my list," Cole says.

"Neither do I," McDonald acknowledges.

"The same scenario for everything I have listed under four-six also applies to the six-four combination," Kenne continues. "So what have we got here?"

"Total confusion," Cole quips.

"Exactly," Kenne responds. "As I've said before, we're in one hell of a mess here. Even if we get lucky and guess right on the day and time of his next murder, we still won't know where it's going to happen."

"Lieutenant, can I make a suggestion?" McDonald asks.

Kenne nods his head at her and says, "Go ahead."

"This Domino creep and his would be clues are driving all of us up a wall. Why don't we tackle this from another angle?"

"What angle is that?" Kenne asks.

"Maybe we should try and find this maniac from information in arrest records."

"That's a great idea, Mac," Kenne congratulates her. Then he chuckles and smiles at her.

"You've already thought of it, haven't you?"

"I've had Singleton and Trop working on it since we've been assigned the case," Kenne informs her. "So far they've come up with zip, nadda, nothing. And, I've got Josh on the streets looking for any angle we can use. Maybe we're on the wrong track but I still think the clue to our killer is in those dominoes. We need to keep working on it and find the answer. And find it fast."

There's a knock on the door.

Kenne yells, "We don't want to be disturbed, unless it's really important like we've got Domino in custody."

Ignoring Kenne, the door opens and Harley is standing in the doorway. He walks into the office and hands Kenne a stapled stack of papers.

"You might find that important," Harley informs him.

Kenne looks at the top page and asks Harley, "What's this?"

"That, my friend, is information about dominoes. I think the answer to the domino killer is somewhere in those pages," Harley answers pointing to the stack of papers.

Kenne looks at the stack of papers and asks Harley, "You got this off the internet, didn't you?"

Harley nods his head.

Kenne yells, "Sam. Get in here?"

Sam rushes in and stands in front of Kenne's desk. Kenne hands him the papers. Sam looks at the top page and shakes his head.

"Yeah," Kenne says in a firm voice.

Sam shrugs his shoulders and pleads, "I never thought of it."

"Make copies of this for everyone in the squad. I want them to read it from cover to cover and we'll get together in the afternoon. Three o'clock should give all the slow readers plenty of time."

****

It's three o'clock and Kenne's squad has gathered in the squad room. Everyone is there except Detective Bradley who is out on assignment. They are all seated at their desks. Kenne and Harley enter the room from his office. Harley takes a seat at the table behind the domino 'Line of Play'. Kenne walks in front of the table and sits on the far edge away from Harley.

"I take it everyone has read the domino information packet that Sam gave you," Kenne says to start the meeting. "My good friend Harley there seems to think the secret to Domino's identity is somewhere in those pages. I tend to agree with him if for no other reason that Domino has access to that same document and its part of his game.

"I want each of you to dissect every paragraph of that report and see if we can come up with something. Don't dismiss any detail. The answer to Domino's identity might be somewhere in those pages.

The telephone on Sergeant Singleton's desk rings. He quickly answers it and says, "Los Angeles County Sheriff's Department, Homicide Squad. This is Sergeant Singleton."

Singleton listens intently to the voice on the other end. Before he hangs up he thanks the caller.

Singleton looks toward Kenne and informs him, "They just found another body. Domino has struck again."

Chapter 4

Double Six

It took Kenne about twenty minutes with siren blaring and lights flashing to get to the crime scene in an apartment building parking lot in the vicinity of Wilshire Boulevard and Western Avenue. The parking lot was already swarming with Los Angeles city police, Sheriff Department officers, Fire Department ambulance personnel and the local media. Also on hand was County Coroner and forensics expert Arnold Fong.

Fong is a very short, thin Chinese man with thin facial hair on his chin that looks like a beard. It's the only hair on his head.

He is standing over a sealed body bag in a parking space and talking into his Smartphone. Kenne walks over to him and puts his right arm around Fong's shoulders and greets him, "You know we've got to stop meeting like this, Arnie."

Fong shuts off his Smartphone and says, "What a wonderful idea."

"What have we got here?" Kenne asks.

Fong bends over and unzips the body bag and opens it. Kenne looks down at the corpse.

"We've got a thirty to thirty-five year old Japanese female. She was stabbed four times in the torso and clubbed six times in the head. She was moved here after she was slain. All indications show that the attack took place over there."

Fong points to a parking space about forty feet away.

"Why would he move the body?" Fong asks.

Kenne looks down and sees the number 46 painted at the foot of the parking space. Kenne shakes his head.

While still looking at the painted number he asks Fong, "Do you have any idea of the weapon that was used?"

"A tire iron. He stabbed her with the pointed end and clubbed her with the blunt end and left it over there."

He points to the same parking space as before.

"Another instrument of death to add to my collection," Kenne sighs.

"It's in my car. I'm going to run it for prints."

"Good luck," Kenne responds. "Get it to me when you're finished with it."

Then he asks, "Any idea about the time of death?"

"I'd say about one o'clock this afternoon."

"Forty-six hours," Kenne mumbles to himself.

Kenne looks around the parking area, shakes his head and mumbles to himself once again, "No security cameras."

Detective McDonald walks up and informs Kenne that the man that found the body is pretty upset because he knew the lady.

Kenne instructs her, "Get as much information out of him that you can. The works."

"He said her name is Anna Kawasaki and she lives alone in number twenty-eight," she informs Kenne.

Detective McDonald looks around and notices the number 46 painted at the parking place.

She looks at Kenne and says, "Forty-Six."

"Yeah. Four-Six." Kenne says without showing any emotion.

Fong interrupts and says, "By the way. I've got something for you."

He reaches into his pants pocket and pulls out a domino.

"This was in her right hand when I got here," he says handing the domino to Kenne.

Kenne looks at the domino. The two sides are six and six. He shows it to McDonald, and says, "Double Six."

"And victim number six on the horizon," McDonald says shaking her head and frowning.

****

Kenne Narration: "Alicia was only mildly upset when I called her and cancelled our cold pizza for dinner date. She completely understood but made me promise to call her tomorrow. She was also sympathetic to my dilemma. What is this maniac trying to tell us with the double six domino? Is he going to strike again in six days at six o'clock? Or in sixty-six hours? Or in six times six which is thirty-six hours? Detective McDonald is right. He's playing a game with us and he's winning. He's definitely winning and I hate it."

"How many more bodies, Kenne?" Captain Manning screams.

"Don't ask me, Ray, ask that sick son-of-a-bitch out there," Kenne responds in an angry voice.

The two men are sitting in Kenne's office with the door closed. They look each other in the eyes and stare for a few moments.

Kenne breaks the silence, "Look Ray, I've got the entire squad on this. We're doing what we can."

"I know. I'm sorry for raising my voice," Ray apologizes. "It's just that a lot of pressure is coming down on me from upstairs."

"Yeah, I know," Kenne says. "We've got a lot of pressure on our shoulders, too."

"What's the last domino he left?" Ray asks.

"Six and six on each side. Double six.

"Any idea what it means?"

"It could mean anything," Kenne answers. "I've got the entire squad working on possible scenarios."

"Keep me informed," Ray instructs Kenne as he opens the door and exits the office.

Just as Ray leaves Kenne's office Detective Ramirez sticks his head in the doorway and announces, "There's a Doctor Goldstein here to see you."

"Send him in."

Kenne stands up and walks around his desk and as Doctor Goldstein enters his office he greets him with a firm handshake.

"What's it been, two years, Marv?" Kenne says opening the conversation.

"More like three," Goldstein answers.

Kenne tells the doctor to have a seat as he sits on the edge of his desk.

Doctor Marvin Goldstein is a police psychiatrist with the Los Angeles Police

Department. He's sixty-two-years old and rather pudgy around the middle. He is here at Kenne's request.

"I suppose you know why I called you?" Kenne states.

Goldstein nods his head and answers, "Domino."

"What can you tell me about this guy?"

"He's not your ordinary serial killer. He plans every slaying with meticulous precision and he leaves those dominoes for at least three reasons. First, he wants to make sure he gets credit for the murder. Second, he's treating his murder spree as a game of profound wisdom. He wants to show the world that he has a genius mentality even though he possesses a sick mind. Third, he wants his so called fifteen minutes of fame and he's getting that and even more with the media attention he's drawn. Actually, the dominoes that he leaves with the victims aren't really clues but more of a tease. He's taunting you and your squad."

Kenne hands Goldstein the domino packet that Harley brought him.

"We seem to think the clue to Domino's identity might be in this information about the game," Kenne informs him.

Goldstein looks at the front page for a moment and hands it back to Kenne.

"It's a possibility, but I doubt it" Goldstein says. "Get me a copy. Maybe I can find something in there."

Kenne and Goldstein talk over old times for about ten minutes like they were long lost brothers. As Goldstein gets ready to leave he encourages Kenne that eventually Domino will make a mistake and he would catch him.

****

It was the morning of June 24th, a Monday, twelve days since Domino's last murder. This was supposed to be Kenne's day off but he cancelled it because of anxiety feelings that Domino was going to strike again, today. He had spent the night at Alicia's and she had already left for work when Kenne woke up.

Kenne was in the kitchen, dressed and about ready to leave when his cell phone rang. It startled him. He looked at his watch before he answered the phone. It was seven-twenty-seven. A sick feeling came to his stomach that someone on the other end was calling to tell him Domino had struck again.

"Yeah," Kenne said answering the phone on the fourth ring.

"Lieutenant, this is Sam," the voice on the other end said.

"What is it?" Kenne asks.

"You asked me to give you a wake-up call at seven-thirty."

Kenne sighed with relief and said, "I forgot. I'm up. I'll be in soon."

Kenne hangs up the phone, and shoves it into his pants pocket. He takes one last sip of Alicia's fabulous tasting coffee sitting on the kitchen counter and heads for the door.

Kenne Narration: "Six days ago my squad was on edge, including me, wondering if Domino was going to strike that day. Much to everyone's relief it turned out to be a quiet day. Today is the twelfth day from Domino's last event and I'm very apprehensive that today's the day he's going to strike again. Everyone in the squad has read Harley's domino report ten times over and more. We've also held three conferences and nothing jumps out in that report that would lead us to Domino's identity. I've scheduled another meeting for ten o'clock this morning and have invited Harley and Doctor Goldstein to attend."

****

The conference started a few minutes after ten. All the squad members were in attendance except Detective Bradley. Kenne decides to start the meeting without him. Everyone is seated at their desks with Harley and Doctor Goldstein sitting behind the table displaying the dominoes and weapons. Kenne is sitting on the edge of the table facing the squad members. He is holding Harley's report in his hands.

"You all know that big man sitting behind me," Kenne says opening the conference. "The good looking gentleman sitting to his right is Doctor Marvin Goldstein. He's a psychiatrist that works with the Los Angeles Police Department. He specializes in the psyche of the criminally insane."

Goldstein raises his left arm as a hello signal to the group.

"Harley," Kenne continues. "On page six of the report under the heading 'Variations and game play,' it states that many versions of the game start with a double side domino like a six and six, five and five and so on. Yet, Domino started his so-called game with the three and five sided domino. Do you have any idea why?"

Harley explains, "It's true that many versions of the game start with a double-sided domino. However if none of the players have a double-sided domino a game can be started with the next-highest domino like the five-three. It's my guess that Domino picked a hand that usually consists of seven dominoes from the bone yard and the five-three was the highest domino. So he started his game with that particular domino."

Sam asks, "Are the rest of those dominoes on the table part of his original hand?"

"Highly unlikely," Harley answers. "The probability of picking seven dominoes that can match would be rare."

Goldstein interrupts, "It's most likely he picked his next domino after planning his next murder. Similar to planning two or three moves ahead in a chess match."

"Exactly," Harley says in agreement.

"Doctor Goldstein, is Domino a copy-cat from the past," Detective McDonald asks.

Goldstein laughs and then answers McDonald's question.

"He's not from the past. He's here now and very much real. As far as him being a copycat, let me explain. A true copycat serial killer usually follows the original as close as possible. However, with Domino, he's using the idea from the fifty's serial killer and expanding on it. So in the true sense he's really not a copycat but an imitation or extension. It's my opinion that he's finishing what Albert Hill started."

"Do you think he's going to use up all twenty-eight of his dominoes?" Detective Cole asks.

"Probably so," Goldstein responds. "That's why the sooner he's caught the better."

"Let's examine what we've got here in Harley's report," Kenne says interrupting the question and answer session.

"We've all read through it a number of times so let's review what we've come up with so far," Kenne says as he opens his notepad. "In Friday's session we've decided the possible answer to Domino's identity is in the History section, Rules section or Footnotes.

"What do you think, Marv?" Kenne asks Goldstein as he turns toward him.

"If you think that's where the answer is, it's as good a place to start as any," Goldstein answers.

"Do you think we're on the wrong track?"

"My expertise is analyzing psychotic killers. Not catching them."

As Kenne is about to continue his cell phone in his pants pocket rings. He pulls it out, opens the lid and looks at the screen. Detective Bradley's cell phone number appears.

"Excuse me," Kenne says as he answers the phone. "Detective Bradley, how nice of you to call. I hope you're bringing donuts."

"Lieutenant, I've got some bad news for you," Bradley says.

In an alarmed voice Kenne asks, "What is it?"

Bradley explains why he is late and Kenne hangs up his phone and sits silent for a moment.

"What is it?" Singleton asks.

Kenne shakes his head and says, "Meeting adjourned. Mac, come with me."

Chapter 5

Double Carnage

Kenne Narration: "Detective Bradley's news wasn't just bad, it was horrifying. Yes, Domino had struck again. When Mac and I got to the scene it was a blood bath. The manager of the Sixth Street Motel and his wife were bludgeoned to death. County Coroner Fong was already on the scene and taking a break at the doorway of the manager's office."

Fong greets Kenne with, "It's another bad day in L.A."

Kenne walks past him without saying a word and enters the motel's office while Mac waits outside. There was blood spattered all over the floor. He walked very carefully across the room and around the counter so he wouldn't step in any blood. The entrance door to the living quarters was open and he stepped inside.

Detective Bradley is sitting at the kitchen table with his head in his hands. He looks up as Kenne approaches him still walking carefully around the blood stains in the area. They both look at each other in silence for a few moments until Kenne breaks the mood.

"Tell me about it."

Bradley shakes his head and relates the story how he was first on the scene.

"I was driving to the office for your meeting and I pass this motel and my subconscious reads the sign, '6th Street Motel.' I didn't pay any attention to it until I get two blocks away. Then it hits me, '6th Street Motel' on Sixth Street. Double Six. I slam on the breaks and make a u-turn thinking it's just a coincidence. It's probably nothing. I pulled into the parking lot and noticed the office front door was open.

"I walked up to the door and noticed blood on the floor. I pulled my gun out and entered the office slowly, expecting … well, expecting anything. As I entered the living quarters I saw a man's body covered in blood lying on the floor over there in front of the couch."

Kenne looks to where Bradley has pointed. A zipped body bag is lying on the floor in front of the couch.

Bradley continues, "I could tell from the streak marks of blood on the floor that his body was dragged inside here. I looked in the bedroom and a women's naked body was lying on the bed drenched in blood. Then I went to the car and called it in. I waited for backup to get here and then I called you."

Coroner Fong walks into the room and tells Kenne, "I'm waiting for the wagon to take the bodies to my lab. I'll call you with the results."

"Today!" Kenne firmly states.

"Within three hours," Fong says as he hands Kenne two dominoes.

Kenne looks at them and says, "Sure."

He turns toward Joshua and says, "I'll see you in my office in about an hour."

Kenne leaves the room and walks outside. Four media vans are parked in the street. One of the reporters, a female, and her cameraman rush over to Kenne and she asks, "Can you tell us what went on inside? Is it another attack by Domino?"

Kenne looks around and sees a number of other reporters and cameramen gathering.

After pausing for a moment he says to all of them, "I'll have more information later this afternoon. I'll hold a press conference at four o'clock in the conference room in Westwood."

Kenne motions to Mac to go to the car. Kenne follows her and they drive away.

****

The first floor conference room is packed wall to wall with media personnel including television cameras. It was standing room only. The podium has a great number of microphones propped up waiting for Kenne. He enters the room and walks to the podium. Captain Manning and Sergeant Singleton follow him in and stand nearby.

Kenne starts the conference, "Let me make this clear. This is not a question and answer session. I will be giving you an update on the Domino serial killer case. Yes, Domino struck again this morning with more deadly mayhem. We have double carnage as he committed two murders. I cannot tell you the victim's names because their next of kin has not been notified as yet. We have made some progress on determining Domino's identity and we have identified persons of interest. The information as to who they are is classified at this time. Thank you all for coming."

Kenne walks away from the podium and exits the room. Captain Ray Manning follows him out of the room. Kenne is walking down a corridor with Manning trailing behind.

"Persons of interest?" Manning asks.

Kenne stops and turns toward Manning and says, "I had to give them something, Ray, or they would give our department some really bad press."

Manning looks at Kenne, shakes his head and says, "I suppose you're right, but I don't like it."

****

Kenne is standing at the table with the 'Line of Play' dominoes and staring at them. He is the only one in the squad room. He reaches into his suit coat pocket and pulls out the two dominoes Coroner Fong had given him at the last scene of the crime. He looks at them in his hand for a moment and then sets them on the table. The first domino's sides are six and two. Kenne slides the domino under the six and six domino with the sixes touching. The second domino's two sides are two and blank. Kenne slides that domino facing to his left with the two's touching. He looks at the dominoes for awhile trying to make some sort of sense out of the numbers.

Sergeant David Singleton enters the squad room and walks up to Kenne and stands next to him. He looks at the dominoes and then glances at Kenne.

"You look like hell, Lieutenant," Singleton says breaking the silence.

"You're no beauty yourself," Kenne chides.

"I mean you look exhausted."

"I guess I am," Kenne responds. "My sleeping habits haven't been too good lately."

Actually, Kenne has only been averaging about four hours sleep a night for the last three weeks. It didn't matter if he was spending nights alone at his place or at Alicia's. Sound sleeping was hard to come by. In fact, Kenne has been trying to stay away from Alicia as much as possible because of the nasty moods he's been in from the lack of sleep and the dead ends in the Domino case. He has deep feelings for her and the one thing he didn't want to do was alienate her.

"You need to get away from all this and put it out of your mind. Come on, I'll buy you a beer."

"I don't need alcohol in my system. I need some sleep."

"A few alcoholic beverages will probably make you sleep like a baby, tonight," Singleton says trying to educate Kenne on the sins of alcoholic beverages.

****

The Westwood Sports Lounge is walking distance from headquarters. Kenne and David were lucky to find two seats next to each other at the bar. Happy hour meant two for one, so they both ordered two draft beers. The bartender knows David because he frequents the establishment on a regular basis along with other Sheriff Department personnel.

The bartender serves the four beers to Kenne and David and says, "I saw you on television awhile ago. You guys sure know how to dodge a bullet."

He turns and walks away before Kenne or David can say anything in response.

"A wise guy," David states.

"Everyone's entitled to an opinion," Kenne responds in a tired voice.

"I put Fong's report on your desk. Did you read it?"

"Yeah, I did," Kenne answers him. "This time the magic number is six, just as we figured. Arnie gives the times of death at around six a.m. Domino's instrument of death was a claw hammer with a six inch head. Guess how many times he struck each victim?"

"Six," David answers after taking a long swallow from one of his draft beer mugs.

"You read the report!"

"At least you still have your sense of humor," David commends Kenne.

The two men labor over their beers and get involved in small talk for the next thirty minutes. David finishes his two beers first and orders two more. Kenne still has half a mug left and declines a refill. David slides one of his two new mugs of beer in front of Kenne.

"The beer I promised you," David says with a chuckle.

"Last of the big time spenders," Kenne remarks.

David finishes his beer and announces, "I have to run. Marcie's fixing dinner."

David stands up, pats Kenne on the shoulder and disappears amongst the throng of people standing and watching a Dodger's game on the giant screen television.

Kenne sits at the bar and is zoning out. Not even screams of excitement from the throng watching the baseball game draws his interest even though he's a Dodgers' fan. A few minutes later a very comely young lady sits down in the vacated seat left by David.

"I couldn't wait for your friend to leave," she says to Kenne.

Kenne turns his head toward her and asks, "And you are?"

"My name is Giana Lee. I've been watching you since you came in."

"You poor thing. You must be bored out of your wits," Kenne says sarcastically.

Giana leans toward Kenne and whispers, "Actually, I think you're hot."

Kenne Narration: "I'm thinking about walking back to the office, pulling out the cot from the supply room and spending the night there. I'm ready to keel over from exhaustion and this dazzling vision of beauty is making out with me. Where's a Viagra tablet when you need one? I'll play coy and see where she goes with this. I only hope the subject of money doesn't come up."

"I suppose you say that to all the handsome men you meet," Kenne responds to her purported pickup line.

"You figured it out fast. You're good," she complements Kenne.

"What are you drinking?" Kenne asks.

"Oh, no. I've had enough for one night."

They both stare at each other in the eyes. Kenne could swear he saw twinkles in her eyes. Giana breaks the silence.

"I've seen you before. You're a movie star," she says attempting to flatter Kenne.

"No, you've got me mixed up with that pretty face that looks like me."

"I know I've seen you before," she states firmly. "What do you do?"

Not wanting to tell her he's a cop, Kenne states, "I'm a civil servant."

Giana smiles and those twinkles appear in her eyes again.

"I know where it was. I saw you on television earlier. You were on the news."

"Now you really do have me mixed up with that other pretty face," Kenne says evading her statement and trying to lead her astray.

Giana snickers and gives Kenne a soft punch on the shoulder.

"You're a cop," she says. "A Captain, or something like that."

"Lieutenant," Kenne corrects here.

"You're after that lunatic serial killer. The one that's leaving chess pieces with his victim."

"Dominoes."

"I've never slept with a cop," Giana announces changing the subject.

Kenne looks at her and smiles.

"When you change the subject of a conversation you sure pick a dilly of a topic."

Giana leans over and whispers in Kenne's ear, "Like I said, I think you're hot. Really, hot!"

****

The next morning.

Kenne Narration: "Even though I was on the verge of complete exhaustion, Giana gave me amazing energy. After making love at her place I passed out into a deep sleep. I was out for hours. About nine to be exact. I woke up to Giana's sky blue eyes staring at me. They still had those twinkles in them."

"I hope this isn't going to be a one-nighter," she says.

Kenne doesn't answer her but reaches out and gently caresses her bare breasts.

"Again," she says raising her eyebrows.

"What time is it?" Kenne asks.

"I'm not sure. Around eight, eight-thirty"

Kenne sits up quickly and says, "I'll take a rain check."

Kenne gets out of bed in a rush and starts to get dressed.

"I'll make coffee," Giana volunteers.

"I don't have time. I'm late."

"Will I see you tonight?" Giana asks.

"I don't know. I mean, yeah, I want to see you again but other things are more important right now. You understand."

"I'll give you my phone number. Call me," Giana pleads.

Before Kenne slips his shoes on he falls back on the bed. He grabs Giana and gently pulls her naked body on top of his and plants a long, wet kiss on her mouth. She returns the action.

"I'll cash in on that rain check soon," Kenne whispers in her ear.

While Kenne puts his shoes on Giana writes her phone number on a slip of paper along with the words in big print, RAIN CHECK.

Chapter Six

Solution in the Numbers

It's a little after ten when Kenne walks into the office. Sergeant Singleton is sitting at his desk and is the first to see Kenne.

Singleton looks at his watch, points at it and says, "I told you a few beers would make you sleep like a baby."

Kenne smiles at him and responds, "Yeah, you've got a real winner there. You should copyright it."

"Oh, Lieutenant, your buddy, Harley, is waiting for you in your office," Singleton informs Kenne.

Harley is sitting in Kenne's chair with his feet up on the desk.

"Are you comfortable?" Kenne asks.

"Not really. The chair is too small," Harley answers as he stands up.

Kenne walks around the desk and sits down while Harley grabs a chair from the corner of the office, slides it towards Kenne's desk and sits down.

"Much more comfortable," Harley says.

"What's up?" Kenne asks. "Why are you here?"

"I'm here to apologize to you."

"For what?"

"For leading you astray."

"Leading me astray?" Kenne says in a quizzical voice.

"I'll explain. I've been doing a lot of soul searching and thinking how I can use my sports psychology experience in helping you identify the domino killer. At first I thought the information was in the game of dominoes, its history and like that. Then it hit me last night out of the blue. Domino isn't playing a game. He's invented a new sport. He's using the dominoes as a smoke screen and a plea for help. The solution to Domino's identity is in the numbers."

"In the numbers?" Kenne asks.

"The numbers on the dominoes," Harley apprises him. "Those dominos he's leaving is the smoke screen. He's following a pattern with them to lead you down a dark alley. Actually, it's a sports activity to him. He's setting you up similar to Ali's rope-a-dope. Only he knows what the dominoes mean when he leaves them and it's a one-in-a-million shot you can figure it out before the next victim is murdered."

"I've already figured that out," Kenne responds. "And the plea for help?"

"The numbers on the dominoes is the plea for help. Put them together in the right order and it will lead you to him. He wants to get caught. The numbers could mean anything. A telephone number, social security number, address, credit card number and like that. The numbers are probably jumbled. But to him they make sense."

Kenne looks at Harley with wonderment and asks, "How in hell did you get so damn smart?"

****

Kenne asked Harley to submit a written report on his theory. Later that day Kenne called Dr. Bernstein and asked him to come to his office. About twenty minutes later Bernstein walks into Kenne's office.

Kenne hands Bernstein the report and says, "Read this."

Bernstein pulls up a chair, sits down and reads Harley's report.

"His theory has a lot of merit," Bernstein tells Kenne. "He could be on the right track here. However, I have the feeling there's more to it than that."

"Any ideas what?" Kenne asks.

"Not a clue. Lieutenant, you need to understand that we're not dealing with an ordinary serial killer."

"You've said that before. But there's one thing they all have in common."

"What's that?" Bernstein asks.

"Sick minds."

Bernstein nods his head in agreement.

Kenny rises from his chair and walks to the office doorway.

"Sam," he shouts and then walks back behind his desk and sits down.

Upon hearing his name, Sam rushes into Kenne's office.

"We're going to run the numbers on the dominoes," Kenne instructs him. "I want to see every possible sequence of numbers for telephone numbers, social security numbers, credit card numbers and whatever other numbers there are that anybody can think of. Start with the three-five sided domino and its total of eight and continue with the rest of them like that. I want the numbers like … like yesterday. You got it."

Without saying a word, Sam rushes out of the office.

"You've got more than twenty numbers," Bernstein informs Kenne. "Do you realize how many number sequences you're going to get and how long it will take to check them out?"

"Yeah, I know. It's an impossible job but we've got to do something."

Kenne picks up the receiver from the telephone on his desk and punches a number.

"Ray, I need a computer expert and I need him now," Kenne says into the receiver.

"What for?" Ray asks.

"I'll explain later."

****

"You heard me right," Manning says into the telephone. "I need the best we got and I need him now."

Ray pauses for a moment as the voice on the other end is speaking.

"What do I need him for?" Ray says for Kenne's benefit. "To use the words of a distinguished Lieutenant, I'll explain later."

Ray hangs up the telephone receiver.

"Sheriff Unger," Kenne states, positively.

"A very unhappy Sheriff Unger," Ray informs Kenne. "Now, are you going to tell me what this is all about?"

Kenne explains Harley's theory, the task he gave to Sam and why he needs a computer scientist.

"I used the wrong adverb in describing you as a distinguished Lieutenant to Sheriff Unger. You're a bizarre Lieutenant. And you don't need a computer scientist, you need a mathematician. An Einstein."

"You're probably right, Ray." Kenne agrees. "But, hey, Harley's theory sounds rational to me. And, Goldstein says it has merit."

"When you get the numbers, how many extra people are you going to need?"

"I have no idea," Kenne answers. "That will be your decision. You're the Captain."

"If this doesn't work we're going to have a lot of questions to answer," Ray firmly states. "And I place emphasize on the we."

"Let's hope we can get lucky and it won't come to that," Kenne responds.

Chapter Seven

Too Many Numbers

Sheriff Unger sends a young computer scientist, Eric Perry, from the main office. He's in his late twenties and he's wearing a light blue t-shirt with the American Flag emblazoned across the front, green shorts and sandals; no socks. He also has about a three days growth on his face.

"Nice outfit," Kenne remarks. "K Mart special?"

"Your Captain Manning told me what he wants me to do. It will probably take hours. I'm dressed for comfort."

"Sit down," Kenne directs him.

Eric places a black case on the desk and sits down.

Detective Hartenstein enters Kenne's office and sits down in a chair.

"Detective Hartenstein has already started running the numbers," Kenne starts the conversation. "I've come up with a protocol for the two of you and I want it followed to the letter, understand."

Both men nod their heads as Kenne hands them each a sheet of paper. The two men look at the paper and start reading.

"This is going to take days, not hours, and create thousands of number possibilities," Eric remarks.

"For your information, we're getting some help. The white pages people are going to work with us and identify Los Angeles County phone numbers from our list. Cell phone providers will do the same. The California Franchise Tax Board will identify county residents from social security numbers. I asked them to supply us with single taxpayers only, for now. The DMV will help with driver's license and plate numbers. Bank account and credit card numbers will be more difficult because of the large number of providers so we'll leave them for last."

"What about the alphabet?" Eric asks.

"What do you mean?" Kenne responds with a question of his own.

"Replacing the numbers for letters. Like A for one, C for three, etcetera," Eric explains.

"Don't you think we've got enough with the numbers alone?"

"I guess so," Eric answers.

"Let's not complicate things anymore than they already are. At least for now. Sam, keep me informed of the progress every three to four hours."

****

Kenne calls Detectives Cole, McDonald, Ramirez and Tropazinni and Sergeant Singleton into his office. McDonald and Singleton are sitting in chairs, Ramirez is standing at the closed door and Cole and Tropazinni are standing at the wall nearest to Kenne's desk.

"I don't believe the Ruffin murders were the only reason the double six domino was left with Anna Kawasaki's body," Kenne says to open the meeting. "I've convinced myself that Domino killed the Ruffin's so he could leave two dominoes to escalate the game. The double six domino was just a smoke screen."

"Seven murders," McDonald says. "Isn't that enough escalation?"

"I've got this sick feeling in my stomach that Domino is planning something extremely violent," Kenne informs the squad. "That's what I mean by escalating the game."

"And what he's been doing isn't extremely violent?" Trop interrupts."

" I'm convinced that the six/two side and two/blank side dominoes left with the Ruffin's are linked together to form one clue. Six-two and two-blank are linked in that order in 'The Line of Play' and they're linked together in that same order to clue us in on Domino's next adventure.

"Two days have gone by and he hasn't appeared. Therefore he's going to strike on the sixth day after the Ruffin killings. That's Tuesday of next week. It's going to happen at 2:02 or 2:20 that day."

"A.M. or P.M.?" Cole asks.

"It could be at either time."

"What about the blank?" Ramirez asks.

"I don't think it means anything. It's just a blank," Kenne responds.

"Lieutenant, I think you're wrong," Mac positively states.

"Oh. Do you have a more plausible theory about all this?" Kenne politely asks her. "We'd all like to hear it."

"Not about your theory. About the blank. I think the blank is a substitute for zero."

Kenne looks at Mac for a moment and then says, "Now do you all see why I keep her around?"

They all chuckle.

"Okay, let's assume the blank means zero. Then we're dealing with the numbers six, two, two and zero. Anybody have any ideas how a zero fits in here."

"The zero could fit on the end of the 2:20 time," Singleton professes.

"I don't think so," Kenne says. "Every number on the previous dominoes has had some significance. Just using the blank side to finish off a time of day doesn't make any sense to me."

"Let's put the four numbers together in a different order and see what we come up with," Ramirez suggests.

"No, I think the Lieutenant is right about the numbers," Mac states firmly. "We need to keep them in the same order as they appear in the 'Line of Play'. Six, two, two, zero."

"Any idea what that could be?" Kenne asks the group.

They all are silent for a moment.

"How about an address?" Kenne asks.

"It could be an address," Singleton agrees.

"Maybe its Domino's address," Cole pipes in.

"But, what street?" Mac asks.

"It's not Domino's address," Kenne asserts in a positive voice. "It's where his next attack is going to take place. Mac, you and Lamar get a list of all streets in the county with a six-two-two-zero address."

"Lieutenant, that could be thousands," Cole dejectedly states.

"I know. Too many numbers again, but hopefully we can eliminate most of them and concentrate on those that might make sense," Kenne replies.

"I've got a friend that works in the County Tax Collectors office," Mac proclaims. "I'll see if he can get us a list of addresses before the day is over."

"Have them broken down between residential and business if possible," Kenne suggests. "What are you waiting for? Go."

Mac leaves the room in a rush and Lamar starts to follow her.

"Where are you going?" Kenne asks.

"You said I should work with her."

"Sit down. We're not finished here," Kenne barks at him.

Lamar sits down in the chair Mac has just vacated.

"Another development is about to come down and I don't like it," Kenne says in a resounding tone. "About an hour ago I received a telephone call from a Ben Marcus. Anybody here ever heard of him?"

They all shake their heads.

"He's an entertainment agent. He has a client named Tony Deerfield."

"The actor?" Lamar blurts out.

"One and the same. It seems that Molly Ruffin was his cousin and he's very upset about what happened to her. In fact, he's so upset that he's going on live television at six o'clock tonight to offer a one-hundred thousand dollar reward for the arrest and conviction of Domino."

"That's big trouble," Singleton apprises everyone. "We're going to have every lunatic in the county calling us to turn in everybody they hate. It's got the handwriting of a nightmare."

"You're right on the money, David. That's why I want you in charge of interrogation of those lunatics. Who knows maybe you'll come up with a lead."

Singleton sits back in his chair and shakes his head continuously with a very sad look on his face. Detective Ramirez reaches out and places his right hand on Singleton's shoulder. Kenne notices the gesture.

"Don't look so distraught," Kenne says. "Ramirez and Trop are going to help you."

"Isn't there any way to stop Deerfield?" Singleton asks.

"I talked to Marcus for forty-five minutes trying to convince him that his client was making a big mistake. His response was 'I work for Deerfield, not you'."

Detective McDonald enters the room and gives Kenne a thumbs-up sign.

Chapter Eight

Business Doesn't Mix with Pleasure

Kenne Narration: "Once again, at the end of the day I am worn out. It's Friday and I promised Alicia I would spend time with her this weekend. She wanted to spend the weekend at Big Bear, Palm Springs or a place like that. I talked her into spending the weekend at my place. It's not Palm Springs but the view of the sunset from my Beverly Glen Boulevard apartment is outstanding and there are a number of good pizza joints in the area. She was sold on the idea, probably because she just wanted to be with me. At least that's what I'm thinking."

Kenne picks up Alicia at her apartment. She is wearing a tight sweater that once again highlights her upper body curves. Kenne doesn't notice anything else because his eyes are fixed on her upper body as she gets into his unmarked black police cruiser and flips a brown and black duffle bag onto the back seat. Kenne is sitting sideways in his seat facing Alicia. After settling in she leans over and kisses him on the cheek.

"I haven't seen you for days and that's all I get is a peck on the cheek," Kenne says in a depressed voice.

"That's all you get because I haven't seen you in days," Alicia responds. "If you want more, you're going to have to earn it."

"I can do that," Kenne says not taking his eyes off of her. "Oh yeah. I can earn it."

"Where are we going for dinner?" she asks.

"Don't beat around the bush," Kenne answers. "Just tell it like it is. You're hungry."

They both look at each other and laugh. Alicia leans toward Kenne and they embrace for a long minute with a hug and wet kiss. Kenne pulls away from the curb after Alicia releases her hug. They sit silent for a few minutes before they start a conversation. Alicia poses a volatile question to start things off.

"Are you making any progress on the Domino case?"

"Sure. His grandmother turned him in about an hour ago."

"Very funny," Alicia responds to Kenne's sarcastic remark.

"And how was your week?" Kenne asks.

"Just like any other week. Boring as hell. You never answered my question about dinner."

"I thought we'd go to my place and I'll put a couple filets on the grill and add cinnamon topped sweet potatoes and asparagus spears smothered in toasted bread crumbs as accompaniments."

Alicia sighs and says, "You sure do know how to capture a girl's heart."

"I'm working on it," Kenne responds along with a wink of his right eye.

They arrive at Kenne's apartment after dealing with rush hour traffic for thirty minutes. Kenne grabbed the two filets from the refrigerator and tested them with a fork to see if they were thawed and ready for the grill. While he was doing that Alicia walked up behind him, put her arms around his chest and rested her head on the back of his neck.

"The filets are not quite ready for the grill," Kenne informs Alicia. "They're about forty-five minutes away from being completely thawed."

"Gee, I wonder what we can do to occupy our time for forty-five minutes," Alicia responds to the information.

****

Kenne had placed his cell phone on the counter near the thawing filets. Sure enough the phone rang while he and Alicia were occupying their time in bed. Kenne paid no attention to the ringing but Alicia was a bit distraught that he had not shut it down. However, it didn't damage the mood.

After they finished making love Kenne started cooking the sweet potatoes and asparagus while Alicia jumped into the shower. While Kenne was cooking he listened to the message Sam had left on his cell phone.

"Lieutenant, this is Sam. We're finished running the first set of numbers. Eric and I are getting bleary eyed from looking at the computer screens so we're calling it a night. We'll get back on it first thing in the morning. I've got a rep from the white pages coming in at nine to help us edit the numbers. I also have a number sequence of possible valid social security numbers. We'll run them in the morning. Enjoy your evening."

Alicia enters the kitchen area just as the message is finishing. She kisses Kenne on the cheek and then walks into the living room.

"Show me how to work the television remote," she says as she picks it up from a couch end table.

A moment later Kenne takes the remote from her and asks, "What do you want to watch?"

"The news would be good."

Kenne turns on the television using the remote and then finds a newscast for Alicia.

"I've got to get the filets ready," Kenne says as he rushes back to the kitchen.

While he's fussing over the filets he can hear the newscast. George Wyatt, who has a time slot on the program is just starting his nightly broadcast.

"Good evening, I'm George Wyatt and this is The Gripe. Two days ago, just after the domino serial killer struck again and murdered Patrick and Molly Ruffin, Detective Lieutenant Kenne Quintcannon of the Los Angeles County Sheriff's Department held a short news conference and didn't allow any questions from the media in attendance. And there was many of us." …..

Upon hearing his name, Kenne immediately rushes into the living room to listen closely to what George Wyatt has to say.

….. "At that time he said that his department has persons of interest regarding the possible identity of the domino serial killer. My gripe is, if that statement is true, why has there been no traffic at the sheriff's office in Westwood regarding the apprehendsion and interrogation of these so called persons of interest. Are there really persons of interest or is Lieutenant Quintcannon pulling the wool over the public's eyes? And why is it taking so long for the Sheriff's Department to track down this demented killer? I have made several phone calls to Lieutenant Quintcannon's office seeking answers to those questions and more. I have yet to receive a response from any of the messages I have left."

Wyatt pauses, shakes his head and continues.

"Lieutenant Quintcannon, the public is scared out of its wits. As am I. I beg you. Please, no more smoke screens. It's time to let us know what's really happening. I'm George Wyatt and this has been The Gripe."

Just as Wyatt is signing off, Kenne's cell phone rings. His first thought is to let it ring because he knows its Captain Manning calling. However, he decides to answer it.

"Quintcannon."

"Lieutenant, this is Captain Manning," the gruff speaking voice on the other end says.

Kenne hates when Ray uses formal titles instead of first names. He knows that he's really angry.

"I recognize your voice, Captain," Kenne responds. "If you're calling to find out if I saw that jackass Wyatt's newscast, I did?"

"That jackass has a lot of pull downtown. He's going to cause us a lot of trouble, if he hasn't already," Manning informs Kenne.

"Look, Ray. I'm not happy about what he had to say but since when do we have to report our investigative strategies to the media? And besides the more press they give Domino, the more active he's going to be. Serial killers feed off of attention."

"We're going to have to face this problem Monday morning," Ray says. "Think about how we're going to respond to that jackass' gripes."

Ray hangs up his phone on the other end.

"That was your boss," Alicia says. "He's mad, isn't he?"

"He'll get over it," Kenne responds.

Kenne's cell phone rings again. He looks at the number coming through and recognizes it as Harley's.

Kenne answers the phone, "You were watching."

"Yeah, I was watching," Harley agrees with Kenne's unique way of answering his phone.

"I can't talk now. I'm in the middle of cooking dinner for myself and an astonishing beautiful guest. I'll call you in the morning."

Kenne hangs up the phone and returns to preparing the meal for the two of them. After finishing the accompaniments he asks Alicia for her help in grilling the filets.

Before she agrees she says, "I have a question to ask you."

"Go ahead," Kenne encourages her.

"How did you come about to have such a weird spelling of your first name?"

"If I tell you, you won't believe it."

"Try me."

"My mom told me what happened. It seems on the day I was born my father was filling out the birth certificate form and left the name line blank because he decided that mom would be responsible for choosing my name. He gave her the form and then left for work. The name line asked for last name, then first name with the middle name at the end. Mom started filling out the form and when she got to the first name she thought for a moment and then chose Kenneth. As she was writing the name the pen she was using ran out of ink after writing K-E-N-N-E. She set the form and pen down on the tray table next to the bed and dozed off. When she woke up the form and pen were gone. One of the nurse's aides had picked up the form thinking mom had finished it and turned it in to be recorded. That's the whole truth and nothing but the truth, so help me God."

"I believe it. Nobody it their right mind would make up a story like that. Now what can I do to help?"

"I need someone to hold the cooking fork," he answers.

Kenne hands the fork to her and picks up the tray that the filets are sitting on. He walks to the sliding doors at the west end of the living room and Alicia follows close behind. Kenne slides the doors open and they both step out onto the veranda. Alicia immediately notices the spectacular sunset.

"Wow, what a view," she says in wonderment.

"You get used to it after awhile," Kenne says matter-of-factly as he starts up the propane gas grill.

****

Kenne Narration: "The weekend with Alicia was certainly one to remember. There was a lot of good but too much bad. First, the good. Spending time together gave us the opportunity to really know each other. What we like. What we don't like. And what we have in common besides an attraction to each other which, of course, leads to sex. And, believe me, the sex was … well let's just say out of this world. Now, the bad. The constant ringing of my cell phone caused way too many interruptions during our intimate time together. It really annoyed Alisha and I wasn't happy about it either. I tried to explain to her that this was part of my job and she needed to cope with it. On the drive taking her home late Sunday night she told me that she wanted some time to think about continuing our relationship. When she got out of the car she said to me and I quote 'business doesn't mix with pleasure and I don't know if I can handle it.' She was sobbing when she said it."

Chapter Nine

Busy Work

Kenne enters the squad room at about 7:45 Monday morning and it is bustling with activity. In fact, nobody notices him as he makes his way to his office. Captain Manning is waiting for him in the office.

Ray greets him with a gruff, "Good morning."

"Good morning?" Kenne greets him in the form of a question. "From the sound of your voice I don't think your having a good morning."

"Actually, it started last night," Ray says. "I received a phone call from a very unhappy Sheriff Unger. It seems he and Mayor Kennelly would like to meet with us this morning about Wyatt's Friday night broadcast and the reward that damn actor has offered. They'll be in my office at ten."

"I don't have time for their political bullshit," Kenne adamantly complains.

"Either do I," Ray agrees. "But Sheriff Unger is still our boss. So be there."

Ray exits Kenne's office in a huff and slams the door behind him. It startles everybody in the squad room and they sit silent for a moment. As Ray makes his way through the room everyone stares at him.

As he reaches the door he turns and yells, "What are you all staring at? Get back to your busy work."

He slams the squad room door behind him.

Sam opens the door to Kenne's office and enters. Just as he does, Kenne, who is standing nearby, turns his head and sneezes.

"He's Grumpy and you're Sneezy," Sam comments.

"And who are you, Snow White?" Kenne responds sarcastically.

Kenne sneezes again and takes a handkerchief out of his pants pocket and blows his nose.

"Are you coming down with a cold?" Sam asks.

"No, I'm allergic to wise guy cops," Kenne continues with his sarcasm.

Sam nods his head with a grin on his face.

"What have you got for me?" Kenne asks.

"A nightmare," Sam answers. "We've got thousands of telephone and cell numbers and about three thousand socials. It's going to take weeks to go through the names and the numbers."

"Where do you and the boy wonder think we should start?"

"I don't have the faintest idea and I don't think he does either."

"Start with the socials. Compare names on the socials to felons. See how many matches you come up with," Kenne advises.

Sam leaves the office and Kenne follows him. Sam makes a right turn to his desk and Kenne turns left and heads for Detective McDonald's desk.

"I only want good news," Kenne says to Mac.

Mac looks up at Kenne and says, "There's about six-hundred 6220 addresses in the county and around 200 of them are business or industrial addresses. I also had my friend run addresses with just the 622 numbers. There's 550 of them and about half are business addresses."

"That is good news," Kenne agrees. "I thought there would be much more and running the 622 numbers was a good idea."

"Also, this morning I asked him to run the addresses by city and zip code. I figured it would be easier to check out the addresses with that information."

"Good thinking. Start checking them out. Start with possible addresses near Domino's assaults. Maybe we'll get lucky."

Kenne starts to walk away and stops. He turns and looks at Mac then at the table with the domino 'Line of Play' exhibit. He walks over to the table and stares at the dominoes.

"Zip codes," he barks out. "The son-of-a-bitch is tormenting us with the simplicity of zip codes."

Detective Cole is sitting near Mac's desk. They look at each other and both of them open their eyes wide. Sam also looks up and then rushes over to Kenne's side just beating Lamar and Mac by a split second.

"Sam, get us maps of every zip code in the county. Mac, you Lamar, Dave, Alphonso and Trop work on possible zip codes from the domino numbers and match them up against the maps. Everything else is on hold. Domino is going to strike again, tomorrow. I can feel it in my gut. We need to figure out in which zip code and then find the street address."

"Lieutenant, all zip codes in the county start with a nine," Sam says. "There's no nine."

"Then let's assume the nine is silent. Use it as a fixed number."

****

Captain Manning greets Sheriff Unger and Mayor Kennelly with firm handshakes and then offers them a seat.

"Where's your boy wonder, Quint-cannon?" Sheriff Unger asks.

Manning flips a switch on his intercom and says, "Lieutenant, Sheriff Unger and Mayor Kennelly have arrived. You want to step in here."

There is no answer so Manning leaves his office and is headed for the squad room. Kenne is standing at the table and staring down at the domino 'Line of Play'.

Manning calls him, "They're here."

Kenne turns his head toward Manning and says, "I'll be there in a minute."

Kenne is not happy that he has to waste his valuable time conferencing with two men that he considers egotistical politicians. With that in mind he takes his time before making an entrance into Captain Manning's office. Upon entering the office, Kenne walks past the two politicians and sits on the corner of the credenza behind Captain Manning. He's taking that position so that the two politicians have to look up at him and he can control the conference.

"I believe you know these two men," Manning says to Kenne.

"We've met before," Kenne responds with negativity in his voice.

Mayor Kennelly opens the conversation, "We've got six dead and you haven't got past step one in finding this maniac killer."

"Seven," Kenne says correcting him.

As he does, Captain Manning cringes.

"What?" the Mayor questions.

"We've got seven dead civilians, not six," Kenne answers. "And we have gone way past step one in our investigation. But neither of you would know that because you don't have the slightest idea of how to conduct a criminal investigation."

"Don't get smart with me, Lieutenant," the Mayor shouts as he leans forward in his chair and points a finger at Kenne. "I could fire you for that insolence."

"I don't work for you. I'm employed by the County of Los Angeles. In other words, I work for the County Board of Supervisors and they're not about to fire me because it would look bad on them and the Sheriff's Department if they did that in the middle of the most important criminal case in the county's history."

The Mayor and Sheriff look at each other and then nod their heads sideways toward each other. The Mayor then sits back in his chair.

"Let's relax here," Captain Manning says breaking into the conversation. "We've got important business to discuss here."

"Lieutenant," Sheriff Unger says in a loud voice. "In your press conference the other day you said that you have persons of interest as to Domino's identity. Is this true or did you lie to the press?"

"No, I didn't lie to them. We do have persons of interest."

"May I ask who they are?"

"Every felon that is on the loose in the county," Kenne answers with disdain.

"You've got to have better communication with the press," Mayor Kennelly says.

"Let me tell you something, Mayor. The more press coverage this psychotic gets the more he'll feed off of it and the serial killing will get worse than it already is. My suggestion to you Mayor is to hold a press conference and inform the media that we are diligently investigating this serial killer and making progress and wait until we are ready to release more information to them."

"Are you making progress?" the Mayor asks.

"Yes, we are."

"Can you tell us how much progress?"

"No. The information we are working on is privileged and you're not on the list to receive it, Mayor. Now, if you'll excuse me, I've got work to do."

Kenne stands up, pats Captain Manning on the shoulder and leaves the room.

"His insolence is beyond reproach," the Mayor contemptuously states. "I don't know how you put up with it."

"I put up with him because he's the best and most dedicated police officer I have ever worked with," Manning extols.

"We need some results pretty fast, Ray," Sheriff Unger demands. "The entire city is panicking."

"My entire squad along with some extra are working overtime to find this maniac. We are using every means possible and following every lead to the maximum," Manning asserts. "Let them do their job without interference and they will solve this case. I'm sure of that."

Sheriff Unger rises from his seat followed by the Mayor.

"I want to be kept informed of the progress on a daily basis," Sheriff Unger asserts.

****

It's close to lunch time and Kenne is leaning back in the chair in his office with his feet on the desk. He is staring at the ceiling as if it has the answers that he's looking for. Detective Ramirez enters the office and immediately notices Kenne's prone position.

"Are you awake?" Ramirez asks.

"Yeah, I'm awake. Just looking for answers."

Ramirez looks up at the ceiling as Kenne sits up in his chair.

"Are there any up there?" Ramirez asks.

"I get enough smartass remarks from everyone else. Don't you start up, too," Kenne responds. "Now, what do you have for me?"

"We're narrowing the zip code numbers down and matching them to possible locations."

"How many?" Kenne asks.

"There's four-hundred and thirty-seven zip codes in Los Angeles county. We've got the number down to just under a hundred."

"Keep working on it. Try and cut that number in half or more," Kenne commands him.

"Oh. And another thing. We've received close to two hundred calls of concerned citizens chasing after the reward that jerk offered on television Friday night. We've got everybody in the county turning in their ex-husbands and boyfriends to their landlords, and pizza delivery boys."

"I knew that was going to happen. Any of them sound serious?"

"Dave says not a one," Ramirez answers rather dejectedly.

"Tell the phone people to have patience. The calls should dwindle down by the middle of next month."

"Very funny, Lieutenant," Ramirez remarks. "Oh. By the way. We're ordering pizza for lunch. You want some?"

"Maybe our pizza delivery boy is the serial killer," Kenne remarks.

Ramirez laughs as Kenne stands up and pulls his wallet out of his back pocket and lays a twenty-dollar bill on the desk.

"I can taste it already. Pepperoni with extra cheese."

Ramirez picks up the twenty-dollar bill along with a slip of paper hidden under it. He looks at the slip and smiles.

"Rain check with a phone number," Ramirez says joyously. "Looks like the Lieutenant, is back in action."

He hands the slip of paper to Kenne and then leaves the room. Kenne looks at the slip of paper and smirks.

"I forgot about this," he says to himself.

****

Kenne and the squad are standing around the table looking at the dominoes 'Line of Play'. Lamar and Trop are chewing on the last of the pizza.

"We've cut the zip code list down to thirty-three possible zones," Mac informs everyone.

"How sure are you?" Kenne asks.

"Pretty sure."

114

"Pretty sure?" Kenne repeats in the form of a question.

"Well, we're about sixty to seventy percent sure."

"That's not good enough," Kenne says with a bit of disgust in his voice.

"Lieutenant, some of the zip codes are interesting," Lamar says as he finishes chewing on the last of his pizza. "They're in the heart of the city and each one covers a small area."

"What are you trying to say?" Kenne asks him.

"I think we should concentrate on those zip codes."

"How many are there?"

"Ten or twelve."

Kenne looks at Lamar and then nods his head.

"That's as good a place to start as any I guess. Get a list of all buildings with 6-2-2 and 6-2-2-0 addresses in those zip codes."

Kenne turns to walk back into his office when Detective Bradley enters the squad room. Bradley holds the door open and a short, old man walks in. Kenne looks at him and starts to walk away then after a brief moment he realizes who the old man is.

He walks toward him and quizzically says, "Mario Gianelli? I'll be damned. What's it been, twelve, thirteen years?"

"Closer to fifteen you bizarre moron," Mario answers.

Gianelli was one of Kenne's favorite instructors at the Police Academy. Kenne loved to torment him with bizarre murder scenarios during class time. That is why Mario dubbed him with the moniker 'bizarre moron'.

The two men hug and then Kenne looks at Bradley and asks, "Where did you find him?"

"It's a long story," Bradley responds.

"Give me the short version," Kenne pleads.

"I was riding my bike down near the Santa Monica Pier when I spotted this group of old men ….."

"Seniors," Mario interrupts.

Bradley continues, "….. group of seniors in the park playing dominoes. So, I wandered over and started to watch. After a bit this old ….. er senior asked me if I was interested in the game. At that point I told him who I was and why I was watching. Then, he introduced himself and said that he knows you. He also said that he might be able to help us. So, here we are."

Just as Bradley finishes his story Mario notices the 'Line of Play' dominoes on the table. He walks over and looks at them and scratches his head. Kenne walks over behind him and suggests they step into his office.

Kenne and Mario talk over old times for a few minutes and then Kenne updates him on the Domino case. Mario suggests they take a good look at the 'Line of Play' on the table outside Kenne's office.

About twenty minutes have gone by and Mario had been standing in front of the table looking down at the 'Line of Play'. All this time he has been rubbing his chin as if it would make him think better.

Meanwhile, the squad is trying to eliminate some of the addresses in the favorable zip codes.

"Why is he standing there so long without moving?" Lamar asks Trop.

"He's eighty-years-old. You should move that fast when you're eighty," Trop answers.

"That's not funny," Lamar responds.

"I thought it was."

Kenne walks over to Mario and asks him, "Any bright ideas?"

"I believe so," Mario answers. "Bring me those maps of the central Los Angeles area."

Mac overhears Mario and brings him the desired maps and spreads them out on the table. Mario thumbs through them and pulls one out.

"How many dominoes does a player gather from the bone yard at the beginning of a game?" Mario asks Kenne.

"If I remember correctly from reading about the game, seven," Kenne answers.

"Right. And how many dominoes do you have here?"

Kenne counts them and responds, "Seven."

"That's also right. How many pips are there on the dominoes?"

Kenne adds them up and says, "Fifty-one."

"Is fifty-one divisible by seven?"

Kenne does some quick math in his head and answers, "No."

Mario looks at him with a surprise on his face and states, "I never was any good at math. Let's forget about the pips for now."

What are you driving at?" Kenne asks.

"Seven. The magic number is seven," Mario positively states. "Zip code nine-triple ought-seven. That's where he's going to pull off his next caper."

Mario holds up the zip code 90007 map.

"Are you sure?" Kenne asks.

"One can never be sure of how a psychotic thinks, but it's as good of place as any."

Mac takes the map out of Mario's hand and the squad starts to search for possible six-two-two and six-two-two-zero addresses in the 90007 zip code.

Kenne and Mario return to his office and do some more reminiscing. Shortly after that Kenne takes Mario to lunch and then drives him back to the Santa Monica beach.

Chapter Ten

Follow the Numbers

Kenne Narration: "It was good to see Mario and reminisce about my time at the Police Academy. He hasn't changed much except to get older. It also took my mind off of the breakup with Alicia. On the ride back to the office I kept going over possible scenarios that we haven't covered. Other ideas kept popping into my head but none of them seemed feasible except for other uses of the number seven. I wasn't exactly sure what, but more thinking had to be done."

Kenne arrives back at the squad room and asks everyone to gather around the 'Line of Play' table.

"We still need to follow the numbers and not miss a beat," Kenne says. "Sam, what have you got for me?"

"We found seven matches with felonies on the social security numbers run," Sam reports. "One of them is dead and two are incarcerated. We've got the last known addresses on the other four and one is a female."

"Get me all the information you can on the dead man," Kenne orders.

"Lieutenant, you think the serial killer is a dead man?" Sam asks in a surprised voice.

"Just get me the information," Kenne orders then pauses for a moment before he continues. "Dave, you, Josh, Alfonso and Lamar form four squads of three uniformed officers each, obtain arrest and search and seizure bench warrants from Judge Wellington and bring the four in for questioning and do it all. If they've moved, find them. Trop, get me the yellow sheets on all of them."

"Lieutenant, what should we charge them with?" Detective Cole asks.

Kenne thinks for a moment and then answers him, "Trespass on the arrest warrant and weapons violation on the search and seizure."

The four detectives look at each other in amazement and then obtain the addresses from Eric and leave the squad room.

"What about the phone numbers, Sam?" Kenne asks.

"We're still working on them but we've got the list narrowed down to about a thousand."

"Come on," Kenne yells. "We're running out of time, here."

Kenne and Sam look at each other for five seconds.

"I'm sorry," Kenne apologizes. "I know you've been working hard on this"

"That's okay, Lieutenant. I understand."

"How's zip code 90007 coming, Mac?" Kenne asks.

"There are no six-two-two-O addresses and seven six-two-two's. Four of those are residences and three are businesses," Mac replies.

"Let's concentrate on the three businesses. Notify L.A.P.D. we need their help with surveillance on those businesses starting at midnight, tonight. Come see me after that. For those still here, meeting adjourned."

****

Kenne Narration: "You're probably wondering along with Sam if I think a dead man is our serial killer. How silly can you be to think such a thing? Actually, I have a reason to get as much information on him as I can. Let me explain. Before I enrolled in the Police Academy I spent two years at UCLA studying criminal law. At the end of my second year one of my professors gave us an assignment of writing a term paper about the commission of a crime with a solution at the end. I chose murder as the subject. The first thing you investigate in a murder case is motive. My scenario had an important politician murdered. The murder weapon, a gun, was left at the scene of the crime supposedly to lead police to suspect the owner. That's exactly what the police did. Through weapons registration the police identified the owner. When they went to arrest him they found out from his brother that he was killed in an automobile accident two days prior to the crime. Of course, the murderer didn't know this so the crime was solved by investigating who had a motive for the killing. It turns out that the dead politician was having an affair with the wives of both the dead man and his financial advisor. The financial advisor knew of the affairs and therefore had the motive. The case was solved when the dead man's wife pointed the finger at the financial advisor because she knew about the other woman. To make a long story short, the murderer was the financial advisor's wife because of jealousy. So, you never know what part of an investigation can lead you to the perpetrator. Anyhow, the professor gave me an F on the term paper and flunked me. He never told me why but I think it was because I never explained how the financial advisor's wife obtained the murder weapon. Anyhow, that's what led me to the life of a dedicated policeman."

While waiting for Mac to return from her assignment Kenne decides to cash in his rain check. He calls Giana's number from his cell and gets an answering machine after four rings. Just as he's about to hang up a voice answers.

"Hello."

"Giana, this is that handsome man with the rain check," Kenne quips.

"I'm sorry, there's nobody here by that name," the voice answers.

"Who's this? You sure sound like her."

"I'm Eliana. Who's this?"

"Just a friend. This is the number she gave me," Kenne says.

"Well it's the wrong number," Eliana answers. "Don't call here again."

Kenne hangs up.

Not long after Kenne hangs up, Mac enters his office.

"I got what you wanted but I had to go through a Captain Shields," she says.

"He's not a nice man."

"I would be shocked if you thought anything else of him," Kenne responds.

"He said he would call you later."

"I can't wait."

Kenne makes a motion with his right hand towards a chair in front of his desk and says to Mac, "Have a seat. I've got something to run by you."

Mac sits down and looks into Kenne's eyes and says, "This case has really got you in a quandary."

"That's what I want to talk to you about," Kenne says confirming her suspicions. "Two things are bothering me. Do you remember Mario saying he wasn't good at math?"

"I do," Mac answers.

"I still have a gut feeling that the number seven in a zip code is the key to Domino's next carnage but I'm not so sure that the zip code 9-0-0-0-7 is where it's going to happen. That would be too simple. I think Mario fell for it because he's not good at math and our psychopath is. Other zip codes containing a derivative of seven are more likely what we're looking for. Like seven plus seven, fourteen; or seven times seven, forty-nine; or the sum of small numbers adding up to seven and still assuming the first number nine is silent."

"You want me to run those numbers?"

"Yes, with Sam and Eric's help."

"What was the second thing bothering you?" Mac asks.

"So far, Domino is winning at his dangerous game. I think we need to turn the tables on him."

"You have any ideas?"

"Yes," Kenne answers with emphasis.

Chapter Eleven

Possible Suspects

Sergeant Singleton assigned Detective Ramirez, because he spoke Spanish, and his uniformed squad to picking up Paulo Dominquez. Dominquez is a convicted felon with three assaults with a deadly weapon charges. His last known address is in Gardena. Ramirez and his squad park in front of a single story residence in two squad cars. The house is run down with two shutters missing on the front windows and two other shutters barely hanging on its hinges. The place looks as if it hadn't been painted in twenty years. The front yard was a sea of weeds and a beat-up 1982 Ford pickup was in the driveway. The house was surrounded by an aging, rusty chain link fence. The gate to the front entrance was missing.

Upon exiting their vehicles Ramirez points to the two uniform sheriff officers in the second squad car and orders them, "You two cover the back and remember we want him alive. If the back door is open, don't enter until we're inside."

Ramirez motions to Baynes, the uniform officer that rode with him to follow behind him. As they approach the front door,

Ramirez can hear the television blaring. It's tuned to a Spanish speaking station. Ramirez knocks on the front door.

"Dominquez, this is the Los Angeles Sheriff's Department. "We'd like to talk to you," Ramirez yells.

"Yo no hablo Ingles muy bueno," Dominquez says in Spanish.

(Translation to English – "I don't speak English so good.")

"Quien eres?" He continues.

(Translation to English – "Who are you?")

Ramirez identifies himself in Spanish. "Me llamo Ramirez. Soy detective con la los Angeles condado alguacil departamento. Me gustaria hablar con usted."

(Translation to English – "My name is Ramirez. I'm a detective with the Los Angeles County Sheriff's Department. I'd like to talk to you.")

"Que pasa?" Dominquez asks.

(Translation to English – "What about?")

"Tengo que conseguir una cierta informacion importante de usted," Ramirez answers.

(Translation to English – "I need to get some important information from you.")

Dominquez opens the door and Ramirez is staring at a large chest wearing a dirty

Raiders' t-shirt. Dominquez is six-feet-five-inches tall and weighs about three hundred pounds.

Ramirez looks up at him and asks, "Podemos entrar?"

(Translation to English – "May we come in?")

Dominquez steps aside and Ramirez and the uniform officer step inside. Dominquez walks backwards into the center of the living room. Ramirez holds up his badge in his left hand and the arrest and search and seizure warrants in his right hand.

The two officers in the rear of the house hear Ramiriez in the living room and they enter through the open back door and walk into the living room with their weapons drawn. Dominquez turns and looks at them as Ramirez explains why they're here.

"Tenemos una orden para su arresto y una orden de busqueda y captora de los locales."

(Translation to English – "We have a warrant for your arrest and a warrant for search and seizure of the premises.")

"Warrant para lo?" Dominquez asks.

(Translation to English – "Warrant for what?")

"Orden de detencion por allamiento. Busqueda y captura de armas," Ramirez informs him.

(Translation to English – "Arrest warrant for trespass. Search and seizure for weapons.")

"Entra illegal?" Dominquez yells loudly.
(Translation to English – "Trespass?")

Cuff him, take him to the car. I'll read him his rights when I get there. Officer Baynes cuffs Dominquez and leads him outside.

"Do it all. Every room," Ramirez instructs the other two officers.

****

Sergeant Singleton and his squad are standing at the door of apartment 312 in a fashionable six-story apartment building on Sherman Way in Reseda, a small community in the San Fernando Valley. Singleton knocks on the door while his companions wait with their back to the wall, out of sight from the door. There is no answer. He knocks again.

A voice yells out, "Who's there?"

Singleton answers, "Mr. Poe, Jason Poe. I'm Sergeant Singleton with the Los Angeles County Sheriff's Department. We'd like to ask you a few questions."

"Questions about what?" Poe asks.

"I don't' want to shout through the closed door and cause you trouble with the neighbors. If you'll open the door I'll explain."

Poe opens the door as far as the chain lock will allow.

"Why can't you people leave me alone. Let me see your badge."

Singleton holds up his badge to the open space.

"Okay," Poe says as he removes the chain and opens the door wide. Singleton and the three uniform officers rush in and Singleton holds up the warrants in front of Poe's face.

"These are warrants for your arrest and search and seizure of the premises. Cuff him Martinez and read him his rights."

As Martinez cuffs Poe's hands behind his back Poe asks, "What the hell is this all about? I'm clean. I've been clean since I got out."

"We need to question you about some illegal activity that you might be involved in," Singleton informs him.

Martinez reads Poe his rights and Singleton looks around for a few moments.

He says to Martinez, "Take him to the car."

Singleton turns to the other officers and says, "One room at a time. Floor to ceiling. Do it all."

****

Detective Bradley and his three-man uniformed squad are sitting in two unmarked police cars – two in each car - on a dead end street in Bell Gardens, a small community southeast of central Los Angeles. Bradley had knocked on the door of the two-story rooming house where Alfred Righetti lives. The landlady told him that Righetti wasn't there and he comes and goes at odd hours of the day and night. After calling in and informing Kenne of what's happening, Kenne orders Bradley to stake out the building in hopes Righetti would soon show.

While on surveillance Bradley, who has a keen eye for detail, makes note of the surrounding area just in case Righetti bolts when they approach him. West of the dead end street is an empty area of about a quarter of a mile long that ends at the 710 Freeway. If Righetti bolted that way, catching him would be a piece of cake because they could chase him in the squad cars.

He looked around and notices there was residential housing in all the other directions. If Righetti bolted in any of those directions, he could disappear in a heartbeat. That would leave Bradley no choice but to call for more recruits.

About twenty minutes later Righetti comes around the corner at the end of the block and walks toward the rooming house.

Bradley knew it was him from the description Kenne gave him on the radio from Righetti's yellow sheet information. Kenne also told him to be careful. Righetti could be armed and dangerous. Bradley passed this information on to his squad members.

"That's him," Bradley informs the uniform officer in his car.

"Let's get him before he goes inside," the officer says.

"No. Let's wait. If we try and apprehend him outside, he could bolt and I don't want to have to chase after him. Let's wait until he gets inside and up to his room. We've got to search the place, anyways."

Bradley waits about ten minutes and then he and his squad approach the front door of the two-story building. Bradley signals for one of the uniformed officers to cover the back in case Righetti tries an escape route out a back window.

The landlady meets them at the door and instructs Bradley which room is Righetti's. Bradley suggests to the landlady that she should leave the house and wait outside until this was over. He then leads the way as he and the two uniformed officers follow close behind. When Bradley gets to the top of the staircase he pulls out his police issued revolver. The two officers do the same.

Bradley whispers to his companions, "I'm going to kick in the door. After I do I'm going to get down on one knee. You two get beside me and enter the room carefully."

The three men move slowly to the door of Righetti's room. Bradley nods his head and the two officers get in position on both sides of the door. Bradley raises his foot and kicks the door near the knob. The door swings open and he drops to one knee, pointing his revolver. The officers peer slowly into the room pointing their revolvers.

Righetti is sitting on the edge of the bed and as the door crashes open he starts to reach for a revolver laying on the night stand.

"No, no, no. Don't make me blow you away," Bradley shouts.

Righetti sits back down on the edge of the bed and raises his hands. Bradley rises from one knee and all three of the policemen enter the room.

"What in hell is this about?" Righetti asks in a loud voice.

Bradley walks over to the night stand and picks up Righetti's revolver and hands it to one of the uniform officers. He then pulls out his badge and warrant papers from his inside jacket pocket.

"You're under arrest for Trespass," Bradley informs him.

"Trespass? What the hell is that?" Righetti shouts.

"Get up and turn around," Bradley instructs.

Righetti rises and turns around. His hands are still raised. Bradley takes a pair of handcuffs out of his jacket pocket and he pulls one arm down at a time and handcuffs Righetti's hands behind him. While doing this Bradley reads him his Miranda rights.

"You have the right to remain silent. Anything you say can and will be used against you in a court of law. You have a right to an attorney. If you cannot afford an attorney, one will be provided to you. Do you understand the rights I have just read to you?"

"Yeah, yeah. I've heard 'em before," Righetti answers in a nasty tone.

Bradley instructs one of the officers to take Righetti to his car while he and the other officers proceed to apply a thorough search of the premises.

Chapter Twelve

Not the Right Answers

Kenne forgot about the wrong number situation when trying to cash in on his rain check with Giana because the persons of interest that were apprehended had to be interrogated. That was more important to him at the moment. He made the decision that he and Bradley would question the three suspects with Ramirez joining in as translator while interrogating Dominguez.

Just as he was leaving for the interrogation center, Detective Cole returns empty handed.

"Lieutenant, that female person of interest Ana Trout's address was a UPS store. The apartment number was actually a rented box number," Cole informs Kenne.

"Did you get any information on her from the clerk?"

"Yes, I did. She rented the box about a year ago from the same clerk that was on duty. She said that she couldn't identify her because when Trout came in she was wearing one of those surgical masks. She told the clerk that she had a cold and didn't want to spread it."

"How did she pay for the box?"

"She paid in cash for one year in advance. Her year is up next month. Oh, and she's never received any mail."

"You did good. I don't think we're looking for a woman, anyhow. We're about to interrogate the other three. Come along. You can sit in and watch."

****

The interrogation rooms are on the fourth floor of the building next to the lockup. Kenne and Lamar take the elevator up to the fourth floor where Bradley and Ramirez are waiting along with two uniformed officers assigned to the jail.

"Neither Dominquez or Righetti fit the description we got from Alicia Jackson but we'll put them through the normal routine. We'll do Dominquez first. Josh, you and I will alternate questions. Ramirez, try and keep up," Kenne instructs his two companions.

They all enter the interrogation room, including Lamar. Dominquez is sitting at a table with his hands handcuffed in front of him. They are settled on the table. Lamar grabs a chair and sits against the wall behind Dominquez. Kenne, Bradley and Ramirez gather around the table but continue standing. Dominquez looks up at them and then turns his attention toward Ramirez.

Dominquez shouts, "Esta es una mierda."

Ramirez translates, "This is bullshit."

"Shut up and answer my questions. I'm in no mood for your bullshit. You got it," Kenne shouts back at Dominquez.

"Callate y responde a mis preguntas. Estoy en nin gun estado de amino para so mierda. Ya lo tienes," Ramirez translates to Dominquez.

"Que en el infieno es?" Dominquez asks.

Ramirez translates back to Kenne, "Who in the hell are you?"

"I'm the devil and I'm going to torment you all night," Kenne responds to the question.

"Soy el Diablo te voy a atormentar te toda la noche," Ramirez translates.

Dominquez shuts up and looks at the ceiling. Kenne bends over and puts both hands on the table to balance himself. He looks Dominquez in the eyes.

"You're in big trouble," Kenne states, loudly.

Ramirez translates, "Usted esta en un gran problema.

"Que tipo de problemas?" Dominquez sheepishly asks.

"What kind of trouble," Ramirez translates.

Bradley jumps in, "You know what you've done."

"Sabes lo que has hecho," Ramirez translates.

"Why don't you tell us about it," Kenne asks.

Ramirez translates, "Por que no nos dices acerca de lo?"

Dominquez says, "Usted me arestado por instrusion illegal."

"Your arrested me for trespassing," Ramirez translates.

After pausing for a moment, Dominquez asks, "Donde iba a hacer esto?"

"Where was I supposed to do this?" Ramirez translates.

"Forget about that. Tell us about the other thing," Bradley shouts.

"Olvidate de eso. Nos hablan de otra cosa," Ramirez translates.

Dominquez asks, "Que otra cosa?"

"What other thing?" Ramirez translates.

Kenne replies, "You know, that nasty thing with the ax."

Ramirez translates, "Sabes negocio desargradable co el hacha."

"No se loque estas hablando. Yo mo he hecho una cosa," Dominquez states.

"I don't know what you're talking about. I haven't done a thing," Ramirez translates.

"Come on. We searched your place. We found all if it," Bradley shouts.

Ramirez translates, "Vamos has. Buscado un hotel en su lugar. Enccontramos todo lo."

"Todo logue?" Dominquez asks.

"All of what?" Ramirez translates.

Kenne leans forward closer to Dominquez.

"The black sweat shirt. The Domino set with the pieces missing," Kenne shouts.

Ramirez translates, "La canisa de sudor negro. El domino con los pedazosque falta."

Dominquez stares and Kenne and then looks at Bradley and Ramirez.

While looking at Ramirez he says, "Espera un momento. Usted piensa soy el asesino de domino?"

"Wait a minute. You think I'm the domino killer?" Ramirez translates.

Bradley answers him, "That's right. We've got you dead to rights."

"El justo. i tenemos muertos para derechos," Ramirez translates.

"Come on Dominquez. Tell us about it," Kenne says in a pleading voice.

"Vienen en Dominquez. Nos hablan de el," Ramirez translates.

Dominquez screams, "Estas demente. Nose nada de esa mierda."

"You're crazy. I don't know anything about that shit," Ramirez translates.

"You're lying. Tell us about it. You'll feel better once you get it out," Bradley yells at Dominquez.

"Esta mintiendo. Nos hablan de el. Se sentira major una vez que usted," Ramirez translates.

Dominquez shakes his head and says, "No puedo desirte lo que no se."

"I can't tell you what I don't know," Ramirez translates.

Kenne stands up erect and places his left hand on Ramirez' shoulder.

"I'm finished with this guy," Kenne says. "Check out his whereabouts at the time of each slaying."

Kenne walks to the door and turns around toward Ramirez and says, "Oh, yeah. Give him his one phone call."

Kenne and Bradley leave the room and stand outside the interrogation room. Lamar joins them a moment later.

"Stay with them," Kenne says to one of the officers standing close by.

He then turns to the other officer and asks him to bring Righetti to interrogation room two.

****

The three detectives are standing around in the interrogation room discussing how they want to handle Righetti's interrogation.

The door opens and Righetti appears in the doorway. His feet are shackled and handcuffs embrace his wrists with a chain hanging down to the shackles and is attached to them. He's dressed in an orange jumpsuit worn by all prisoners. The officer pushes Righetti and he shuffles into the room with small steps.

"What's this all about?" Kenne asks.

"He was causing a lot of trouble so we shackled him," the officer informs Kenne. "If you're smart you'll leave him that way."

The officer leaves the room, shutting the door behind him.

"Sit down," Kenne orders Righetti.

Slowly, Righetti pulls out a chair from the table and sits down. Bradley walks over and checks that the handcuffs and shackles are on tight and Lamar sits down in a chair not far from the table.

Kenne slams Righetti's yellow sheet on the table in front of him.

"Six pages, Alfred," Kenne starts the interrogation. "I've seen yellow sheets with three and four pages, but six pages? That's got to be record."

"I'm a nasty son-of-a-bitch," Righetti snidely says.

"So am I, when I want to be," Kenne wisecracks back.

Bradley shouts, "And, he's a pussy cat compared to me."

"It looks like you're going bye-bye for a long time," Kenne informs Righetti.

"You sending me to Tahiti for a vacation?" Righetti wisecracks.

Kenne laughs and then says, "The illegal goods we found in your room are pretty serious stuff."

"Fifty-five pounds of marijuana, thirty-eight pounds of hashish, eighty-two pounds of cocaine and sixteen different types of firearms," Bradley shouts.

"I'm not saying anything until my lawyer gets here."

"What are you going to pay him with?" Bradley asks. "We've also confiscated your cash booty and the bank book with a hefty sum in it and we're going to freeze the account in the morning when the bank opens."

"What did you find when you stuck your head in the shitter?" Righetti wisecracks.

Kenne reaches out and grabs Righetti's large nose and twists it hard.

"I don't want another wisecrack coming out of your mouth or I'm going to keep twisting until it's as large as a watermelon. You got it?" Kenne says.

Righetti, writhing in pain looks up at Kenne with tears in his eyes.

"You got it?" Kenne repeats.

Righetti nods his head.

Kenne lets go of the nose, smiles at Righetti and says, "Now, let's continue."

"We want to know two things," Bradley says. "Who did you get the stuff from and who are you selling it to?"

"I don't know where it comes from. My cousin gets it," Righetti states.

"What's his name and where can we find him?" Bradley continues.

"You know I can't tell you that. It would be bad for business."

Kenne informs him, "You don't get it, do you? As of six o'clock tonight you've been shut down. Your business is bankrupt."

"He's my cousin, man. I can't give him up."

"Who are you selling the stuff to?" Bradley asks.

"You know. I get around. People know me."

"What kind of instrument of death were you going to use on your next victim?" Kenne asks, changing the subject.

"What?" Righetti says with a quizzical look on his face.

"You heard me."

"I have no idea what you're talking about."

"Where did you hide the domino set?" Bradley asks.

"The what?" Righetti answers.

"The set with the domino pieces you've been leaving with your victims. Where is it?"

"What in the hell are you talking about?"

"You've been playing a game with us and I'm tired of it," Kenne says. "Now it's my turn."

"If this is some kind of game you're playing to make me tell you where my cousin is, it's not working. I'm not giving him up."

"We don't care about your goddamn cousin, you asshole," Bradley shouts. "We want you for those seven murders."

"Seven murders?" Righetti quizzically repeats. "You're out of your mind. I've never killed anybody. Wait a minute. You think I'm that … that domino guy?"

"We know you are," Kenne firmly states. "And you're going to tell us all about it?"

"Hey, I've done a lot of nasty things in my time but nothing like that. You've got the wrong guy."

"Why the cache of weapons?" Bradley asks.

"I sell them, man. I don't use them."

"That's not what this says," Kenne shouts as he points to the yellow sheets on the table.

"Well, I've never killed anyone that didn't need it," Righetti sheepishly admits. "And, besides, I've served my time for that shit."

146

Kenne and Bradley look at each other in despair. Then, Kenne walks to the interrogation room door, opens it and motions to the uniform officer on duty at the door to come into the room. He does so.

"Take him back to the lockup." Kenne orders the officer. "No visitors, except his attorney, if he's got one. We'll be filing felony counts against him in the morning."

Kenne motions to Lamar and Bradley to follow him out into the hall. Kenne walks to interrogation room four and stops at the door.

He turns toward Lamar and orders him, "Do the paperwork on Righetti. I want to file it with the D. A. first thing in the morning."

Lamar heads toward the elevator and Kenne tells Bradley, "Get Poe and bring him here."

****

Kenne is sitting at the table in interrogation room four when Bradley opens the door and escorts Jason Poe into the room. He is handcuffed.

Kenne points to a chair on the other side of the table and tells Poe, "Sit down."

Poe sits down and Bradley sits on the table's corner near Poe.

"Do you know why you're here?" Kenne asks.

"The warrant was for trespassing," Poe answers. "What kind of bullshit is that? What's trespassing?"

"You've been trespassing on private property while on your latest crime spree," Bradley informs him.

"What crime spree?"

"If you don't mind, we'll ask the questions and you're going to provide the answers we want to hear. Got it?" Kenne calmly says.

Poe nods his head.

Kenne opens the interrogation with his first question, "Where were you on Wednesday, April seventeenth at about ten p.m."

"I don't know for sure. Probably at home," Poe answers.

"Was anyone with you?" Bradley asks.

"I live alone. Wait a minute. Wednesday night at ten. That's when my favorite show is on. I never miss it."

"What show is that?" Kenne asks.

"Bronson: American Hero," Poe answers proudly.

"What was the show about?" Bradley asks.

"Let me think a moment. Wednesday, April seventeenth. Oh, yeah. That's the episode where Bronson helps the New

148

Orleans police department ferret out a serial killer."

"How come you know that so vividly? It was two months ago," Kenne states.

"I don't know. I just remember."

"Maybe you remember because you wanted to establish an alibi," Bradley says. "I think you taped the show and watched it sometime later because you weren't home. You were someplace else, like North Hollywood."

"No. I was home I tell you."

"You know we're going to check this out. We've confiscated your TV equipment and forensics is researching the cable box as we speak," Kenne informs Poe.

"You look nervous, Poe," Bradley says. "Is there something in that cable box you don't want us to know about?"

"I've told you the truth. I've got nothing to worry about," Poe answers curtly.

"Friday, May third at three in the afternoon, where were you?" Kenne asks.

Poe looks at Kenne and pauses for a second then states, "That's a work day. I was at work all day."

"What are your hours?" Bradley asks briskly.

"Seven to five and they give me an hour or so for lunch."

"Who's they?" Kenne also asks briskly.

"Where I work. Dobbs Construction."

"What do you do their?" Bradley asks.

"I'm a truck driver. You know. I deliver merchandise and equipment to job sights."

"Then you probably have some time to yourself that can't be accounted for by your dispatcher," Kenne states.

"I don't have any time to myself when I'm at work. They keep me busy all day."

"We're going to check with your dispatcher on your schedule that day," Bradley informs him.

"Go ahead. He'll confirm I worked all day."

"It's not all day that we're interested in. Just where you were at three o'clock," Kenne states.

"Where were you at four a.m. on May twenty-fifth, a Saturday?" Bradley asks.

"Home in bed sleeping. And I was alone."

"How about Wednesday, June twelfth at one in the afternoon?" Kenne asks.

"Working," Poe answers in a word.

"And, Monday, June twenty-fourth at six in the morning?" Bradley asks almost before Poe can answer Kenne's last question.

"Look. I have no idea what this is about."

"Just answer my last question," Bradley shouts startling Poe.

"Six in the morning. I was on my way to work. I start at seven."

"What did you do with the gloves you use?" Kenne asks.

"My work gloves?" Poe asks.

"Surgical gloves," Bradley says.

"I don't have any of those kinds of gloves. Just heavy work gloves. I'm not a doctor."

"We found a lot of incriminating evidence in your apartment. Tell us about it," Kenne says.

"Where do you hide the weapons and the domino set?" Bradley asks almost before Kenne can finish his question.

"Domino set!" Poe shrieks. "Holy shit. You think I'm that maniac serial killer that's been running around loose?"

"We don't think, we know," Bradley states. "The clues you've been leaving have finally caught up with you."

"When and where were you planning your next caper?" Kenne asks. "What does six-two-two-zero mean?"

"I have no idea what you're talking about. I've been clean ever since I got out of Lompoc some five-years ago."

"We're going to keep you overnight, until we can check you out," Kenne informs Poe as he rises from his chair.

Kenne then turns his attention toward Bradley and instructs him, "Take him back to the lockup and have Dave and Lamar check out his alibis first thing in the morning. Oh, and give him his one phone call."

Kenne walks to the door and turns and faces Poe.

"Oh, by the way. We have your computer. We'll let you know what information of interest we find in it," Kenne says.

Chapter Thirteen

The Wrong Man?

It was a quarter to nine when Kenne was finished with his interrogations. They get his adrenaline running and he knows he won't be able to sleep so he heads back to his office and thinks about calling Alicia. He quickly dispels the idea because he doesn't want to make things any worse in their relationship.

Instead he decides to try calling that number Giana gave him again to redeem his rain check. If that was really a wrong number he might decide to go to her apartment.

Giana answers the phone on the second ring with, "Hello."

"Is this Giana?" Kenne asks.

"Yes. Who are you?"

"I've got this rain check that I'd like to redeem," Kenne declares.

"You still didn't tell me who you are."

"How many rain checks have you given out?" Kenne answers with a question of his own.

"Just one," she answers. "I'm just having a little foreplay with you."

"You're cute. How about that redemption?"

"Sounds like a wonderful idea," Giana answers, "When?"

"I'm on my way out the door as we speak."

"I can't wait. Hurry."

Kenne Narration: "Another night of incredibly wild sex had me worn out in the morning. Giana was still sleeping when I woke up. I showered and put on yesterday's soiled clothes. Giana was waking up as I was leaving. I told her that I would call her later. On the way to the office I remembered that I wanted to ask her about that wrong number business. Oh, well. If I forgot to ask it probably wasn't important."

Detectives Ramirez and Bradley and Sergeant Singleton were hard at work putting the finishing touches on their arrest reports when Kenne entered the squad room on Tuesday morning. He went right to his office without stopping to converse with anybody. His first order of business was to call the Sheriff's Department Director of Information, Nikki Cox.

She answered her phone on the first ring, "Good morning, Nikki Cox speaking. How can I help you?"

"Good morning Nikki, this is Lieutenant Quintcannon," Kenne greets her. "I have a little task for you."

"With that case you're in charge of, I doubt that it's a little task but what can I do for you?"

"I need you to set up a media conference for me at noon tomorrow in the Westwood conference room."

"I was right. That's no little task," Nikki says.

"I know you can handle it."

"Noon tomorrow in the Westwood conference room. You got it Lieutenant. Can I tell them what it's about?"

"Just mention my name. They'll know."

A few moments before Kenne finished his conversation with Nikki, Detective Ramirez entered his office. Kenne motioned with his left hand for Ramirez to sit down.

"Here's my arrest and interrogation report on Dominquez," Ramirez says as he hands Kenne the report.

Kenne reads the report and sets it on the desk.

"Lieutenant, if that guy's the domino killer then I'm a Spanish nobleman," Ramirez quips.

"You're no Spanish nobleman," Kenne jests. "File your report in Dominquez' dossier and set him loose if we don't have anything on him."

Ramirez laughs and grabs the report off of the desk. As he exits the room he says, "Why can't I be a nobleman? I'm an honorable and distinguished gentleman."

Kenne laughs and shakes his head.

As Ramirez is leaving Kenne's office Detective Bradley is standing at the door waiting to submit his report on Righetti. Bradley winks at Ramirez as he walks past him. Ramirez stops and looks Bradley in the eyes.

Bradley says, "Honorable and distinguished, yes. A gentleman, I'm not so sure."

Ramirez stares at Bradley for a moment and then both men laugh as Ramirez walks away. Bradley enters Kenne's office and sits down in the chair Ramirez had just vacated. He hands Kenne his report on Righetti.

After reading the report Kenne asks Bradley, "Do you think Righetti is Domino?"

"Not a chance in hell," Bradley answers. "He's a bad dude but not smart enough to pull off that kind of depravity."

"I agree," Kenne states. "Book him on drug and arms possession. I'll talk to the County D. A. about sale and distribution. Dave and Lamar are putting together a report on Poe. As soon as I have it the two of us will team up and interrogate him, again."

****

It was almost noon when Singleton and Cole brought their report to Kenne. Both men had a smile on their face.

Kenne takes one look at their faces and asks, "What have you got?"

"Our serial killer," Singleton brags.

Kenne looks at Cole and throws another question, "Are you in agreement, Detective Cole?"

Cole things for a few seconds and then answers, "Yes, Lieutenant. I believe Poe is the alleged perpetrator."

Kenne picks up the six page report and reads it while Singleton and Cole sit down and continue to gloat with big smiles.

"You've done a good job. I'm impressed. Does Poe have counsel yet?"

"I believe so," Singleton answers.

"Dave, contact his attorney and bring both of them to number one. Lamar, tell Joshua he needs to join me in number one as soon as counsel arrives," Kenne commands.

Both men leave the office and Kenne reads the report once again and highlights certain areas with a yellow highlighter.

****

Kenne has made two copies of the report. One is for Detective Bradley and one for Poe's attorney. He brings all copies to interrogation room one as soon as he is notified that Poe and his attorney are waiting for him.

Bradley has already arrived and he is sitting across the table from Poe and his counselor. Kenne sits down next to Bradley and hands him and the attorney a copy of the report.

"How have you been counselor?" Kenne asks Poe's attorney.

Poe's counselor looks up from the paperwork and into Kenne's eyes and responds, "The name is Rhoda, or have you forgotten?"

"No, I haven't forgotten. But, we need to keep this on a professional level, counselor," Kenne answers her question.

Detective Bradley looks at Kenne and then Rhoda with a quizzical look on his face before he starts reading the report. Rhoda also reads the report.

Rhoda's full name is Rhoda Parson's. She and Kenne had a very hot love affair in the past and the breakup was not amicable. She is a stunning woman with long black hair that highlights her high cheek bones. She is dressed in a woman's gray business suit and a blue ruffled blouse. A red rose is pinned to her suit's left lapel and a visitor label to her right lapel. Her eye shadow, lipstick and makeup have been applied with impeccable care, specially the eye shadow that highlights her light blue eyes. Rhoda works for the Public Defender's office, a position she has held for many years. In fact, she met Kenne on a case she was working.

Kenne notices the red rose and says to Rhoda, "I see things are the same with you."

She smiles at him and then turns her attention to the report.

"You need to inform your client of his rights before we get started, counselor," Kenne states.

While still looking at the report, Rhoda says, "I already have. He'll answer your questions the best he can because he wants to get this over with as soon as possible so he can get on with his life."

"Mr. Poe, do you understand your rights as they were explained to you by your attorney?" Kenne asks.

"Yes, I do," Poe answers.

"Counselor, do you understand why we're holding your client?" Kenne says as he looks Rhoda in the eyes.

"Yes, I understand but I object. Your warrants weren't appropriate."

"Tell it to the grand jury judge and by the way the D.A. will be recommending no bail."

Rhoda grins at Kenne and says, "Let's get on with it."

Kenne starts the interrogation, "Mr. Poe, we've run a series of numbers that are on the dominoes that have been left at the scene of six gruesome crimes. We feel that the numbers on the dominoes are clues to the murder of seven people. We ran possible matching numbers with the California Franchise Tax Board and lo and behold your social security number popped up along with a few others. We then matched those numbers against our files of known felons. Your number popped up again. What have you got to say about that?"

"I have no idea what you're talking about," Poe answers.

"Serial killers are sick people," Bradley breaks in. "Part of their M. O. is that they want to get caught. They want the mayhem to stop. That's why you've left the dominoes at the scene of the crimes."

Poe and Rhoda look at Bradley with surprise.

"You'll have to excuse Detective Bradley. At times he can be over zealous. But, he is right," Kenne interjects.

"There's no need for that. You haven't established a thing," Rhoda says in a loud voice.

Kenne says, "Let's continue. Our forensics lab analyzed your cable box and their findings concurred with our assumption that on April seventeenth you did in fact tape the ten o'clock Bronson show that night. This means your alibi that you were home that night – the same night and time Gilbert Patterson was slain – may not be true."

"What have you got to say about that, Jason?" Bradley asks in an excited tone.

Poe looks at Rhoda and she nods her head that it's okay to answer the question.

Poe answers, "Like I said before, I tape shows late at night in case I fall asleep watching them."

"Do you do that a lot?" Bradley asks.

"Yes. Quite often," Poe answers.

"Then how come our forensics lab found that you only taped three other shows that month?" Kenne asks.

Poe shakes his head and says, "They made a mistake."

"They don't make mistakes, Jason. You taped that show so you could watch it at a later time and use it as an alibi that you were home that night," Kenne explains.

"In other words, your alibi doesn't hold water," Bradley interjects. "You killed Patterson with a railroad spike that night at the time your taped show was running. You know you did it."

Kenne softly says, "Why don't you tell us about it. Start by telling us where you got the railroad spike."

"I've got nothing to tell. I didn't do anything of the sort," Poe answers.

"You don't know anything about driving a railroad spike through Patterson's heart or have you blacked it out?" Kenne says.

"I know nothing about railroad spikes," Poe answers.

"Then let me ask you this," Kenne continues. "If you know nothing about railroad spikes, how come our forensics department found on your computer hard disc that in June, two years ago, you used the internet to get information about them? You deleted the information shortly thereafter. But, as you know, just because information is deleted from everyday use it still stays in the recycle bin on the hard disc."

Poe bends his head down and says nothing.

Rhoda puts her hand on Poe's shoulder and tells him, "You don't have to answer."

"Pre-meditated murder, Poe," Bradley shouts. "The gas chamber, Poe."

"Let's move on," Kenne says.

"No," Poe yells. "Can't you see I'm being set up? Somebody is framing me."

"Now who would want to do that?" Kenne asks.

"I don't know."

"Like I said, let's move on. Did you know that the dispatcher, Mr. Harry Flanagan, at Dobbs Construction keeps very accurate records as to where his trucks are or supposed to be at all times? That's why you are radio dispatched and must check in every hour."

Poe shrugs his shoulders.

"Flanagan told my Sergeant Singleton that according to his records on Friday, May third at three o'clock you were finished with your last delivery and on your way back to the yard. However, you didn't return until five minutes of five. His records also indicated your last delivery was in Alhambra which is a stone's throw from East L. A. where victim number two, Eric Van Horn was stabbed eight times with an eight inch knife."

"Alhambra is a fifteen to twenty minute ride from East L. A.," Bradley interrupts. "Depending on traffic, East L. A. is about an hour's ride to the Dobbs Construction yard." That would give you plenty of time to kill Mr. Van Horn and put you back at the yard around five o'clock."

"No, no. I remember now. I got stuck in traffic on the Hollywood Freeway on the way back from Alhambra. It was a mess."

"You were radio dispatched," Kenne says raising his voice. "Did you call your dispatcher to let him know where you were and what was happening?"

"I don't remember," Poe answers.

"But you remember the freeway being clogged up," Bradley breaks in. "It so happens that Mr. Flanagan's dispatch records show that you didn't call in. That's why you conveniently don't remember."

"Did you check to see if the Hollywood Freeway was indeed backed up that afternoon?" Rhoda asks.

"Actually, we did our homework there," Kenne answers. "The California Highway Patrol and L.A.P.D. have no record of a major delay that afternoon. No accidents. No construction."

"That doesn't mean that there still could have been a traffic backup. The usual Friday mess," Rhoda explains.

"Even so. It would have to one hell of a mess to take two hours to go from Alhambra to the Dobbs yard," Bradley says.

Rhoda sits back in her chair and looks at Kenne first and then Poe.

Bradley continues, "Do you work on Saturdays, Jason?"

"No. The company's closed on week-ends," Poe answers.

"Then you're free on weekends to create mayhem," Bradley states.

"Saturday, May twenty-fifth at four a.m. Where were you?" Kenne asks.

"Probably sleeping," Poe answers.

"Probably?" Bradley shouts.

"I was sleeping. I'm always sleeping at four in the morning."

"Maybe you weren't sleeping on that particular morning," Bradley states. "Maybe you were in downtown L. A. killing poor homeless Willie Jackson with an ice pick. You don't like homeless people, do you?"

"I tell you I was home sleeping, man. I don't have anything against homeless people."

"Where did you buy the ice pick, Jason?" Kenne asks.

"I've never bought an ice pick."

"We're checking retail stores in the areas where you live and work to see if anybody recognizes you purchasing an ice pick," Kenne informs Poe. "Now, do you want to tell us where you bought it?"

"That's a waste of time. I'm telling you, I've never bought an ice pick."

Kenne looks at Rhoda and she returns the look with a wide, eye opening stare. Kenne notices her soft blue eyes that used to drive him into a frenzied state. After a moment he turns his attention back to Poe trying to forget her blue eyes.

"Jason, have you told Ms. Parsons about your felony history?" Kenne asks.

"That's irreverent," Rhoda interrupts.

"I don't think so. You need to know what kind of scumbag you're defending," Kenne states.

"Can I see the yellow sheet?" Rhoda asks as she reaches out with her left hand.

Kenne hands her Poe's yellow sheet and she reads it while occasionally looking up at Poe. After reading it she hands the yellow sheet back to Kenne.

Kenne reads from the yellow sheet, "Nineteen-ninety-nine, domestic violence and assault with a deadly weapon on Diana Poe, your wife. The deadly weapon was an ice pick. He stabbed her once in each leg."

Kenne looks at Poe and disdainfully says, "And you said you never purchased an ice pick."

"I forgot about that," Poe responds.

Kenne continues reading from the yellow sheet, "Sentenced to six years at Lompoc for that. Paroled after serving four-years and six-months."

"Hey, man. She was cheating on me," Poe explains in a loud voice.

Kenne continues reading, "Four months after parole, arrested for stalking Diana Poe, who was then his ex-wife. Served nine-months in county jail. Two years after his release he was arrested once again for domestic violence when he assaulted his live-in girl friend. Served twenty-months in

Lompoc. Arrested again two-years ago for domestic violence on the same girl friend but was released when she decided not to file charges."

Kenne looks Rhoda in the eyes and smiles as he says, "Your client is a real beauty. He's graduated from domestic violence to homicide and we're going to prove it."

"Can I have a few minutes with my client?" Rhoda asks Kenne.

"Kenne gets up from his chair and says, "Five minutes."

Kenne and Bradley leave the inter-rogation room as Rhoda rises from her chair. She starts pacing the floor while gathering her thoughts. She stops pacing and faces Poe from across the room.

"When I asked you about your past, why weren't you truthful to me?" Rhoda asks.

"I didn't think it was important," Poe answers.

"You didn't think it was important," Rhoda repeats sarcastically. "If I'm going to have a ghost of a chance of defending you, you've got to be completely truthful with me about everything."

Rhoda leans on the table in front of Poe and asks, "If you didn't make a side trip to East L. A. on May third, what took you so long to get back to the yard?"

"I made a side trip alright, but not to East L. A.," Poe answers.

"Where did you go?"

"The company frowns on employee's running personal errands on company time. That's why I didn't call in and made the stuck-in-traffic excuse."

Rhoda repeats her question, "Where did you go?"

"West Hollywood."

"Why?"

"I needed to pick up some stuff."

"What kind of stuff?"

"Pot."

"Why didn't you tell them?" Rhoda asks in a disturbed voice.

"Because if I'm arrested for anything, I'm a three-time loser. They'll lock me up and throw the key away."

"And if they find you guilty for being the domino serial killer," Rhoda says looking Poe in the eyes.

Poe nods his head a few times and then looks Rhoda in the eyes and says, "I'm not a serial killer. That's the God's honest truth. If you want me to tell them about my pot purchase, I will."

"No. I doubt that they'd believe you. Let's see what else they've got. I'll call them back now."

Rhoda opens the door and finds Kenne and Bradley standing nearby. She motions for them to return to the interrogation room and everyone takes their original seats.

"Are you on the same page, counselor?" Kenne asks.

Rhoda gives him a sarcastic smile and turns her head a bit.

"On June tenth you really pissed me off," Kenne says continuing on with the interrogation. "You murdered George Harrison around one in the afternoon and interrupted by day off."

"Wait a minute," Rhoda interrupts. "You haven't established that Mr. Poe has murdered anyone and I object to you accusing him as such without concrete proof."

"I'm sorry counselor. I didn't mean to offend either one of you but I think we have enough to use any term I Goddamn well please," Kenne storms back. "Mr. Harrison was clubbed to death with a sawed off baseball bat. We found the bat in a trash dumpster about a block away from the site of the assault. It was quite an expensive autographed bat. Do you know whose autograph was on it, Jason?"

"I have no idea," he answers.

"Mickey Mantle. Do you know who he was?"

"Yeah. He was a ballplayer. I think he played for the Dodgers."

"The Yankees," Kenne corrects him.

"Our forensics lab found some interesting information on your computer regarding that piece of memorabilia. Why don't you tell me about it?"

Poe shakes his head and answers, "I don't know anything about that. I'm not a memorabilia collector."

"Then why did you purchase such an item through the internet two years ago?"

"What?" Poe answers.

"We checked with Action Sports Memorabilia in New York and they confirmed that you purchased a Mickey Mantle autographed baseball bat two years ago in May using your bank account debit card."

"I did nothing of the sort."

"We checked with your bank and received a printout of your bank statement for that month. Sure enough, the item was there in black and white," Kenne informs him.

Poe looks at Rhoda and says, "Honest, I never did that. Someone must have used my account."

"We assumed that would be your alibi," Bradley breaks in. "That's why you made a deposit the day before for the exact amount of the purchase."

Poe sits back in his chair, closes his eyes and says, "Somebody tell me this isn't happening."

"It's happening, alright," Bradley continues.

"Your dispatcher told us on that day you took a load of plaster board to the Alhambra job site and returned back to the yard at ten-thirty," Kenne says. "You then took a load of cement blocks to a job site near Pico and LaCienega. They were finished unloading you at around twelve-thirty. You called the dispatcher and told him you were leaving the job site. You didn't return to the yard until four-forty. Which means it took you over four hours to travel fifteen miles. Plenty of time for you to made a side trip where Mr. Harrison was slain. Or, were you stuck in traffic again?"

"I remember that day," Poe answers. "It was a Monday. I didn't get a chance to eat lunch so I stopped on the way back to the yard."

"Where did you eat, McDonalds?" Bradley asks.

"I think it was a Carl's Jr.," Poe answers.

"Uh, huh. Someplace where a clerk couldn't identify you from any other truck driver," Bradley says sarcastically. "Another perfect alibi?"

"That's the way it was but you guys aren't going to believe anything I say because you're set on hanging this domino shit on me."

Kenne continues, "We have an eyewitness that saw a person of your approximate height and weight running from the scene of the crime. The assailant was wearing a black hooded sweatshirt. Guess what we found hanging in your closet?"

"A black hooded sweatshirt," Poe answers. "Actually, I have two of them."

"I know," Kenne says.

"That doesn't mean a thing. There must be thousands of people with black hooded sweatshirts."

"But only one who committed murder," Bradley says loudly,

Kenne pauses for a moment and looks at Rhoda. She stares back at him.

"Anna Kawasaki was minding her own business, walking to her car in the apartment building parking lot where she lives. This was at about one o'clock in the afternoon on Wednesday, June twelfth. Suddenly, she was attacked from behind and stabbed four times in the torso and clubbed six times in the head with of all things a tire iron," Kenne continues.

Bradley interrupts, "Jason, we searched your car and guess what we didn't find?"

"I lost my tire iron a long time ago."

"Yeah, on June twelfth," Bradley positively states.

Kenne says, "Once again we checked with your dispatcher if he knew where you were at one o'clock that day. He said you went on lunch break at twelve thirty and didn't know where you had lunch. Where did you eat lunch that day?"

"I don't know. Probably at a fast food place, like always."

"You seem to like Mondays and Wednesdays more than other days," Kenne declares. "On Monday, June twenty-fourth, you struck again at the Sixth Street Motel at six in the morning. You bludgeoned Patrick and Molly Ruffin, the motel managers, to death with a hammer."

"What a way to start the week off," Bradley breaks in.

Kenne continues, "There was blood all over. It was hard not to step in it unless you were very careful. Guess what? The perpetrator wasn't. We found foot prints in the splattered blood in the lobby and the living quarters. Forensics reports that the foot prints were made by work boots. Probably size eight and a half. What's your shoe size, Jason?"

"Eight-and-a-half."

"What did you do with the boots?"

"I didn't do anything with my work boots. I've been wearing the same boots for the past nine months. I'm sure you found them when you searched my apartment. Did you find blood on them?"

"We'll ask the questions," Bradley says in a loud voice.

"Jason, let me explain something that's a very serious problem for you," Kenne continues. "Besides the information on railroad spikes that was in your computer, forensics also found two other very interesting and incriminating items. It seems you were researching the web for murder scenarios and you found a newspaper article from the early nineteen-fifties that appeared in the Greenville, South Carolina News. It's about a serial killer that used a railroad spike to kill one of his victims. We found the same article."

Poe looks at Rhoda, shakes his head and says, "I don't know anything about that. That's the truth."

"What else did you find?" Rhoda asks.

"Information on how to make a timing device to set off a bomb," Kenne answers.

"I don't know anything about that, either," Poe says looking at Rhoda. "I'm telling you, somebody is framing me."

"If you're being framed, it's a damn good job," Bradley remarks.

174

"We've covered this before, Jason," Kenne interjects. "What kind of enemies do you have that would kill people just to frame you?"

"I don't have the slightest idea."

Rhoda asks, "When was all this internet information supposed to have occurred?"

"About two years ago," Kenne answers.

"He's been planning this for a long time," Bradley says giving his opinion. "The only thing we don't have is the domino set with the missing pieces. Where are you hiding it?"

Rhoda looks at Bradley with evil in her eyes. Kenne has seen that look before. It's a signal she's getting ready to strike, like a snake.

Rhoda holds up the index finger on her right hand and says in a nasty voice, "Just a goddamn minute, here."

Her words draw everyone's attention.

Rhoda turns toward Jason and asks him, "What was your lifestyle two years ago?"

"After being released from jail, I moved in with my brother and his girlfriend. He was renting a three-bedroom house in Gardena. About that time I went to work for Dobbs. Shortly after that I ran into my ex-cellmate at Lompoc. He was in pretty bad financial shape so my brother let him move in with us. A few months later I met up with the gal who introduced me to my ex-girlfriend. She's a topless dancer at one of those clubs on Highland. Anyhow, she told me where I could find my ex and soon after that she moved in with us. She's the one I had that trouble with."

"Where did you get your computer?" Rhoda asks him.

"It was my brothers. He let me have it when he moved to Colorado. He got a better job there and besides his girlfriend was from there."

"Do you know where your brother got the computer?" Rhoda asks.

"I don't know. He had it when I moved in."

"Who had access to the computer before your brother gave it to you?"

"Everyone who lived there, I guess."

"What are their names?" Kenne asks.

"My brother's name is Alex Poe. His girlfriend is Ginger Young. My ex-cellmate is Victor De La Hoz and my ex-girlfriend's name is Ana Trout."

Bradley has been writing the names down on his notepad and then asks, "What about your ex-girlfriends friend. What's her name?"

"I only know her by her stage name. It's Asia Fantasia. She's Korean."

"Which dance club was she working at?" Kenne asks.

"I'm not sure. There's so many of them. I think it was the Fun and Frolic Club," Poe answers.

There's a knock on the door and then it swings open. Detective McDonald is standing in the doorway.

"Lieutenant, can I speak with you for a moment?" she asks.

"Sure. What is it?"

"Maybe you should step out here for a moment."

Kenne rises from his chair and steps out into hallway with Mac. A few minutes later he re-enters the interrogation room and sits back down in his chair. He is holding a padded envelope in his hand. He looks at Poe and then at Rhoda. He shakes his head and turns his attention toward Poe.

"When did you plant it?" he asks.

Poe answers, "Plant what?"

Kenne dumps the contents of the envelope on the table. It contained a note and a domino. The domino sides are blank and four. Everyone stares at the domino.

Kenne picks up the note and reads it, "I am mailing this to you because I couldn't leave this domino at the scene of today's crime. Buildings don't have a right hand. It's signed Domino."

Rhoda, Poe and Bradley sit silent with quizzical looks on their faces.

Finally, Rhoda asks, "What's going on?"

"Detective Bradley, what time is it?" Kenne asks.

Bradley looks at his watch and informs Kenne, "It's two fifteen."

"Fifteen minutes ago, at two o'clock on the dot, there was an explosion in a six-story apartment complex at 6220 Victory in Glendale. The two dominoes that were left at the Sixth Street Motel had sides of six-two-two-blank or O," Kenne reminds everyone.

Kenne crumbles the type-written note and throws it in Poe's face.

"When did you plant the bomb, Jason? And don't give me any bullshit that it couldn't be you because you were locked up here. There was a timing device on the bomb, wasn't there?"

Poe looks at Kenne and tears start to form in his eyes. He holds his handcuffed hands up to his face to hide the tears.

"Answer him," Bradley shouts.

Poe shakes his head while still blocking his tears.

"I … I don't know anything about that."

"You have access to explosives at your place of work, don't you?"

Poe sits silent.

Rhoda breaks in, "Can't you see he's visibly upset? Can't we end this for today?"

"That's a good idea," Kenne says. "I'm getting tired of looking at this piece of crap."

"Can I see you in private?" Rhoda asks Kenne.

"My office."

Kenne rises from his chair, picks up the domino, crumbled note that landed on the table after striking Poe and the other paperwork in front of him. He leaves the room in a rush.

****

Kenne is sitting on the edge of his desk when Rhoda enters his office.

"Circumstantial evidence. That's all we're dealing with here," she states.

"Tell that to the people that died in that explosion," Kenne responds in a gruff voice.

"Look. You have no tangible proof that Poe was at the scene of any of those crimes or had anything to do with today's bombing."

"Still fighting for the underdog," Kenne states.

"Underdog?" Rhoda responds. "The law says that everyone is entitled to defend themselves in a court of law. That's my job."

"I know that."

They both stop the dialogue and look at each other for a while.

Kenne breaks the silence as he asks Rhoda, "What happened to us?"

She shakes her head and then steps forward and places her head on Kenne's shoulder and hugs him. He returns the hug. After a moment she breaks the embrace and takes one step back and grabs Kenne's left hand. Her eyes are moist with tears.

"I don't know," she answers. "We're both hard headed with strong personalities and set in our ways. Maybe, it just wasn't meant to be."

"I'd like to try again," Kenne states.

"It wouldn't work."

"How do you know if you don't try?" Kenne asks.

Rhoda looks at him with her moist, light blue eyes and tells him, "There's someone else."

Kenne pauses for a moment and asks, "Is it serious?"

Rhoda just nods her head.

The moment is broken when Detectives Bradley and McDonald knock on the door and enter.

"Lieutenant, we should be leaving soon," Mac says.

Rhoda smiles at Kenne and says, "I guess I'll see you in court."

She leaves the office.

Kenne instructs Mac, "Mac, get a car from the pool and meet me out front. And tell

Dave I want him with us. Josh and I will be right down."

Mac leaves the office and Kenne says to Josh, "Sit down. I want to run something by you."

Kenne and Bradley sit down in chairs in front of his desk. Kenne notices two yellow sheets sitting on his desk. He picks them up and looks at them for a few moments. He then hands them to Bradley without saying a word. Bradley looks at them and then raises his head slowly and looks at Kenne.

"Wholly, shit," Bradley says.

One of the yellow sheets has the name Ana Trout on it. The other yellow sheet has deceased stamped across the face. The name on it is Victor De La Hoz.

Kenne shakes his head and says, "This puts a new wrinkle into our case. We've got more work to do."

Bradley hands the yellow sheets back to Kenne and says, "You think Poe was telling the truth about being framed?"

"Actually, I don't think he's smart enough to pull this elaborate crime binge off. I'm inclined to think we might have the wrong man."

Before Kenne leaves for the Glendale bomb site with Bradley he hands Sam the two yellow sheets and instructs him to do a background check on both going all the way back to their date of birth.

Chapter Fourteen

Chaos in Glendale

Victory Boulevard in Glendale is in utter chaos when Kenne, Sergeant Singleton and Detectives McDonald and Bradley arrive at the site of the explosion in their two unmarked squad cars. The building at 6220 is still on fire with three fire engines pumping water on it. There are a dozen or more ambulances and paramedic vehicles blocking the street along with numerous Glendale Police and County Sheriff vehicles.

As Kenne exits his squad car he looks around and notices more than a dozen TV media people and their cameras behind the crime scene yellow tape line. Six Glendale Police Officers are guarding the tape line. A group of injured victims that came out of the building are sitting on the sidewalk and curb across the street from the burning building. They are being tended to by ambulance and paramedic personnel.

Kenne spots Glendale Fire Chief Roland Sparks standing near his vehicle. He flashes his badge at one of the police officers guarding the tape line and ducks under it. He walks over to the fire chief and places his left hand on his shoulder.

"Hello, Rollo," Kenne says.

Sparks turns his head toward Kenne and says, "What brings you out here?"

"Domino." Kenne answers

"What's that got to do with what's going on here?" Sparks asks.

"I received this …" Kenne shows him the domino … "and a note in the mail shortly before this happened," Kenne says as he points to the burning building. "The note said that Domino is mailing the domino to me because a building doesn't have a right hand."

"You mean that psycho is responsible for this?"

"Looks like it. What can you tell me?"

"Best we can figure is that a bomb with a timing device went off in the first floor air ducts above the entrance lobby."

"Dynamite?" Kenne asks.

"More than likely," Sparks answers nodding his head.

"What's the count of injured and fatalities?" Kenne asks.

"Don't know yet. But it isn't a small number," Sparks answers and nods his head toward a line of body bags lying near one of the paramedic vehicles.

"Any idea who owns the building?" Kenne asks.

"A large corporation."

Sparks points to a smallish man dressed in a business suit nearby and informs Kenne. "Dillingham over there is the offsite rental agent and manager."

Sparks' cell phone rings and he answers it interrupting their conversation so Kenne walks over to Dillingham. He introduces himself and flashes his badge.

"This is terrible. I know these people," Dillingham says with a lump in his throat."

"I need you to do me a favor," Kenne says as he hands Dillingham his business card. "I'd like you to email me a list of all the tenants as soon as you can."

"I'll do that for you when I get back to my office."

Kenne takes a moment and looks around at the shocking scene. He counts nine body bags and about thirty victims under paramedic care. He shakes his head and sighs as FBI agent Parker Cunningham flashes his badge at Kenne and introduces himself. Kenne shakes his hand.

"One of your detectives disagrees with my opinion that this could be a terrorist activity," Cunningham says.

Kenne shows him the crumbled note from Domino. He reads the note and hands it back to Kenne.

"A terrorist, no," Kenne answers. "A serial killer. Most definitely."

"This doesn't look like the actions of a serial killer."

"You have no idea what this psycho is capable of."

Cunningham looks at Kenne with a puzzled look on his face. He takes a business card out of his inside jacket pocket and hands it to Kenne.

"Let me know if I can help you."

Just as Cunningham walks away the television news lady from Sixth Street waves for Kenne to come over.

He walks over to her and asks, "What's your name?"

"Deborah Tyler. I'm with KABC."

"Turn your camera off and I'll talk to you," Kenne instructs.

Deborah turns to her cameraman and nods to shut off the camera.

"Is this another Domino incident?" she asks.

"I don't know."

"Then why are you here?"

"This happened in my county. Why wouldn't I be here?"

Kenne smiles at her and walks away. He joins his detective team and instructs Mac and Dave to stick around for awhile and gather as much information as they can. Then go back to the office and check his email for a list of the building tenants and have everyone work on checking their backgrounds. Then he tells Bradley he's going to join him to do some legwork.

Chapter Fifteen

Legwork is a Grind

Kenne Narration: "The hardest part of being a cop for me is the legwork. Checking out information on suspects. Following leads on data and like that. It's time consuming and an absolute grind. That's why I usually have members of my squad take care of this part of an investigation. However, too much is happening and I need to prove to myself whether Poe is Domino or not. Rhoda was right. Everything we've got on Poe is circumstantial. We need to find the domino set with the missing pieces and tie it to him. But where is it? We've searched everywhere that Poe could have hid it. His locker and truck at Dobbs Construction. His apartment and storage bin in the basement and his car. We came up empty everywhere."

Kenne and Detective Bradley arrive at the Dobbs Construction facility just before five o'clock. The grounds take up a city square block just off the 210 freeway in San Fernando. The corporate office is a two-story red-brick building surrounded on three sides by an immaculate kept lawn with flower gardens on each side of the entrance.

They are greeted by a receptionist when they enter the lobby of the building. Bradley shows her his badge.

"Is the General Manager still here?" Bradley asks.

"I believe so."

"We'd like to speak to him."

The receptionist pushes up a switch on here telephone system, picks up a microphone and pages the General Manager. Her voice can be heard throughout the whole facility. A few minutes later a tall gentleman dressed in a suit and tie enters the lobby.

"These men are here to see you, Mr. Firestone," the receptionist says. "They're policemen."

Kenne and Bradley introduce themselves and Firestone shakes hands with them and says, "I suppose this visit is about Jason."

"That it is," Kenne states.

"I was worried about him when he didn't show up for work this morning and no phone call. Then I received a call from a public defender, named Rhoda if I remember correctly. She informed me she was helping him clean up a simple legal matter and he needed some time off."

"Can we go somewhere private?" Kenne asks.

"Sure. My office."

As the three men are walking to Firestone's office he says, "I know about Jason's past legal battles but he's been a model employee since he started here. I mean, we haven't had any problems with him at all."

Upon entering Firestone's office Kenne immediately notices that it is neat and orderly like the front lawn and gardens. There are two chairs in front of a large dark oak desk and Firestone invites Kenne and Bradley to have a seat as he does in the chair behind his desk. There is a large bay window behind Firestone and Kenne's attention turns to the expanse of the company's property from the truck garage on the left to the inventory storage area on the right.

"You've got quite a facility here," Kenne says.

"Sometimes I think it's too big," Firestone replies.

"I would imagine security on a plant this size is quite expensive."

"Actually, I try to keep the costs reasonable and below budget. The owners appreciate my efforts."

Kenne changes the subject by saying, "The reason we're here Mr. Firestone is because we need to get some information from you regarding Jason Poe."

"Me and my dispatcher told the other officer's that were here earlier everything we know."

"There's been some new developments that came up and we need your help."

"May I ask why you're holding Jason?" Firestone asks.

"We can't give out that information," Bradley answers.

"What can I do to help?"

"Do you keep dynamite sticks in your inventory?" Kenne bluntly asks.

"Yes, we do," Firestone answers.

"Who has access to them?"

"My inventory manager and our trained demolition employees."

"Do you keep them locked up?"

Firestone swivels his chair toward the bay window and points to a wooden shack at the far end of the inventory yard and says, "In there."

"Can you call your inventory manager in here?" Bradley asks.

"Sure."

Firestone pushes up a switch on his telephone system, picks up a microphone and says, "Bob Spindler, please report to my office."

After a few minutes Bob Spindler enters the office.

"You want to see me, boss?" he asks Firestone.

"These two gentlemen are police officers and they have some questions for you about Jason."

Spindler pulls up a chair at the right side of the desk, nods his head toward Kenne and Bradley and says, "Gentlemen."

"How often do you take inventory?" Kenne asks.

"At the end of every month. Our chief financial officer insists. We keep perpetual inventory figures and my end of month count must match with the computers or else, if you know what I mean."

"Have you ever come up short on your dynamite inventory?" Kenne asks.

Spindler looks at Firestone and asks, "What's this all about?"

"We've got nothing to hide. Just answer their questions, Bob," Firestone instructs.

"Well, not recently," Spindler answers Kenne's question.

"Not recently," Firestone speaks in a loud voice. "Maybe you'd better explain."

Spindler swallows some saliva and says, "It must be about two years ago come the end of this month. There were four sticks of dynamite missing from an open crate."

"Did you ever find them?" Kenne asks.

"No. They never turned up. I just figured that one of the demolition guys took them for a job and didn't fill out the paperwork."

"What about the inventory match with your computer figures?" Bradley asks.

"I didn't want to get anyone in trouble so I just adjusted my report to match the computer inventory," Spindler explains.

"We'll talk about this later," Firestone says, glaring at Spindler.

"Was Poe working for you then?" Kenne directs his question to Firestone.

"I believe he was. Yes, he was. He started driving for us in the spring of that year."

"Did he ever have access to the shack where the dynamite is stored?" Bradley asks Spindler.

"No. Never."

"Do you keep the shack secured at all times?" Kenne asks.

"Oh, yeah. Under lock and key at all times," Spindler answers.

"How many keys are there?" Bradley asks.

"Two. I have one and Norbert Spencer, our construction foreman has the other."

"Does this Spencer fellow ever give his key to anyone?" Kenne asks.

"I'm not sure," Spindler says with a questionable tone in his voice.

"I am," Firestone interrupts. "Sometimes he gives his key to the demolition crew if he's not going to be around when they need some explosives."

"Yeah. That's right," Spindler agrees. "That's why I figured one of them took the missing sticks without filling out the paperwork."

"Could one of them have left the shack unsecured?" Kenne asks.

"Don't know. It's possible," Spindler answers.

"You know, we also store our fourth of July fireworks in that shack," Firestone states.

"You want to explain?" Kenne asks.

"Every fourth of July we throw a party for all our employees and their families. After dark we put on a fireworks display."

"One of the demolition crew members has been trained in fireworks display and he puts on quite a show for everyone," Spindler adds.

"Is the shack left unlocked during the fireworks show?" Kenne asks.

A concerned look appears on Spindler's face and he says, "You know, it probably is."

"Was Poe at that party?" Bradley asks.

"He sure was," Firestone says. "Who could forget? He was accompanied by his girl friend. She was quite a looker and she wore a

195

very revealing outfit. It was hot that day and she was dressed for the heat."

"Could Poe have left the party during the fireworks display and made his way to the shack, unnoticed?" Kenne asks.

"Sure," Spindler says. "It was dark. Anybody could have gone there and taken those missing dynamite sticks."

As Kenne and Bradley are leaving the building, Bradley says, "I told you he's been planning this for a long time."

****

The Fun and Frolic Club is located on Highland Avenue between LAX and the Pacific Ocean. It is also known as Topless Row. A topless greeter welcomes Kenne and Bradley as they enter the club. Kenne flashes his badge and the greeter covers up her chest with her arms as if she was in trouble.

"We need to talk to the club manager. Is he in?" Kenne asks.

"I'll get him," she answers and walks away.

"Bradley notices her swinging hips and comments to Kenne, "They sure don't make greeters like they used to."

"We're here on business. Try to remember that," Kenne comments.

"I'll try but it won't be easy."

The club manager, Charles Rush meets them at the entrance and invites them to sit at a table in the corner away from the flow of business.

"How can I help you?" Rush asks.

"We'd like to talk to one of your girls. Her name is Asia Fantasia," Kenne says.

"She doesn't work here anymore."

"Any idea where she's working, now?" Kenne asks

"Try the Dreamgirls Club down the road. Last time I heard she was working there."

"The Dreamgirls Club," Kenne says looking at Bradley. "Think you can remember that?"

"It's imbedded in my mind," Bradley answers with a smirk on his face.

"There's something you ought to know," Rush says. "Asia Fantasia is her stage name. Her real name is Kim Park. She's Korean and you can recognize her by the tattoo just above her business end in front. It says 'Park It Here' with an arrow pointing south."

"Cute," Bradley quips.

"One more thing. When you go over there ask for my brother Carl. He's the manager."

Kenne and Bradley stand up and start to head for the door when Rush says, "Let me know when you're coming next time. The drinks will be on the house and I'll fix you up with a couple dancers, if you know what I mean."

Kenne turns and rubs his two index fingers together and says, "Naughty, naughty."

****

A six-foot five-inch, three hundred pound Negro bouncer meets Kenne and Bradley at the entrance of the Dreamgirls Club. Bradley sheepishly shows him his badge and the bouncer glares at him with evil in his eyes.

"We'd like to talk to your manager," Bradley says.

The bouncer continues glaring at Bradley, than he focuses on Kenne and back to Bradley.

A moment later he says in a very soft voice, "I'll get him."

Kenne and Bradley look at each other and Bradley says, "He's in the wrong business. He should be on Monday night RAW."

A moment later the bouncer returns and says, "Mr. Rush would like you to join him. Follow me."

The bouncer leads them to a table in front of the stage. Carl Rush is sitting at the table watching a dancer. He motions to Kenne and Bradley to sit down without taking his eyes off the dancing performer. They sit down with their backs to the stage trying very hard not to notice the topless dancer.

Still watching the dancer, Rush asks, "What can I do for you?"

"Does a dancer that goes by the name Asia Fantasia work for you?" Kenne asks.

Rush points to the stage. Kenne and Bradley both turn their heads toward the stage. The first thing they both notice is Asia's tattoo.

"What do you want with her?" Rush asks, still not taking his eyes off Asia.

While still watching Asia, Kenne answers, "We've got some questions for her regarding a friend."

"You can talk to her when she's finished."

Rush leaves and walks over next to the stage. He picks up a wrap and when Asia is finished with her act she exits the stage near Rush. He hands her the wrap and whispers in her ear. She covers herself up and walks over to the table where Kenne and Bradley are waiting and sits down.

"Did you like my act?" she asks.

Bradley starts to answer and Kenne places his hand on Bradley's shoulder. Bradley turns his head and looks at Kenne who shakes his head.

Bradley closes his eyes for a second and then regretfully tells Asia, "We're not here to socialize."

"Yeah, I know. Carl told me you have some questions about a friend."

"Ana Trout," Kenne says.

"I haven't seen her in years."

"How did you meet her?" Kenne asks.

"I met her at a topless club. She was a dancer."

"What can you tell me about her?"

"We became good friends and after awhile we shared an apartment."

"Do you know a Jason Poe?"

"Yeah. We went out a couple times but he wasn't my type. I fixed him up with Ana and she ended up moving in with him."

"Anything else you know about their relationship?" Bradley asks.

"Yeah. They had some domestic problems and he went to jail. Lompoc I believe. Turned out he was a repeat offender."

"Did you stay in contact with Ana after that?" Kenne asks.

"She moved back in with me for awhile and shortly after that she got into some kind of trouble and they put away for awhile."

"Do you know what kind of trouble?"

"I think she beat up some guy."

"Did she contact you when she got out of jail?" Bradley asks.

"No. But I heard she moved back in with Jason when he was paroled."

"And after that?" Kenne asks.

"I heard she had some more trouble with Jason and she moved back east. Her mother was sick and she went back there to take care of her."

"Where back east?" Bradley asks.

"I'm not sure. Alabama or Georgia."

Kenne and Bradley glance at each other for a few seconds.

"Which was it, Alabama or Georgia?" Kenne asks.

"I'm not sure. I'm not real good at geography."

"Could it have been a big city?" Bradley asks.

"I don't know. Maybe."

"Maybe Atlanta?" Kenne asks.

"That sounds familiar."

"Do you happen to have any pictures of her?" Bradley asks.

"I don't think so."

"Do you think the place where you met might have some kind of promotional photos of her?" Kenne asks.

"I don't know. It was a long time ago. Probably not."

"Can you give us a description of her?" Kenne asks.

As Kenne asks the question Bradley pulls his notebook and pen out of his jacket pocket.

"Yeah, sure. She was a brunette with hair down to her shoulders. Good looking with a dancer's body. She was about two or three inches taller than me."

Asia is five-foot-two.

"Did she have any scars, birthmarks or tattoos?"

"I don't know. I never slept with her."

"Was she still dancing when she moved back in with you after her release from prison," Bradley asks.

"No. She was working at one of those escort services on Wilshire in Beverly Hills."

"Do you know which one?" Kenne asks.

Asia thinks for a moment and then answers, "It had the name Leisure in it but I'm not sure of the whole name."

"Thanks for your help," Kenne says ending the interview.

Kenne Narration: "I told you legwork was a grind."

****

While Kenne and Bradley were on their way to Wilshire Boulevard in Beverly Hills they called Sam and had him find the full name of the escort service and the address. It took him about three minutes.

Leisure Companion Escort Services is located on the ninth floor of an exclusive Wilshire Boulevard office building in Beverly Hills. The security guard at the parking garage entrance refused to let Kenne and Bradley inside because they were not on the visitor's list. Kenne flashed his badge and the guard reluctantly let them pass.

"You need to park on level three," the guard shouts as they drive away.

The view from the window behind owner Barbara Kerrigan's desk was of the heart of Beverly Hills. The sun was setting to the west and created a picturesque scene.

Kerrigan was a pretty lady with a school girl figure in her late forties or early fifties. You could tell she spent time fixing her makeup and eye liner as it was done to perfection. She had long blond hair that flowed halfway down her back.

Kenne flashes his badge without saying a word.

Kerrigan says in a huff, "I run a perfectly legal business. You've got no call to be here."

"We could care less about your business operations," Kenne says to soothe her nerves. "We're here to get some information on one of the girls that used to work for you."

"Which one?"

"Ana Trout."

"Oh, yeah, Ana," she says with a sigh. "She was very popular. Had a lot of recalls."

"Would you happen to have a photo of here in your files?" Kenne asks.

"After one of my girls leaves me I destroy all of her records. I only keep files on my current escorts."

"Did you know she served time in jail and also was detained for solicitation?" Kenne asks.

"I don't do background checks on my girls. That's their business. As long as they stay clean while they work for me I'm happy. Wait a minute. If she's got a record don't you have a photo of her?"

"The one we have in the file is old, she's not wearing any makeup and she has blonde hair which doesn't match current descriptions of her."

"I'll say. She was always a brunette when she worked for me."

"How long did she work for you?" Bradley asks.

"Off and on for about six or seven years, if I remember correctly."

How much money did she make?" Kenne asks.

"That's private information. I'd rather not say."

"I could subpoena your books," Kenne warns her.

"Please, don't hassle me with that shit."

"I need to know what kind of lifestyle Ana was capable of living."

After thinking for a bit, Kerrigan says, "Most of my escorts make sixty to seventy thousand a year. But like I said, Ana was popular. She probably made eighty, maybe ninety"

"Any idea how much she made on the side?" Bradley asks.

"I have no idea what my escorts make from other activities. That's their own business."

"We know that when she left your employment she moved to Georgia to take care of her sick mother," Kenne states. "Do you happen to know her mother's name?"

"Sorry, I don't know her mother's name. And, I don't know that Ana is her real name, either."

"You want to explain that," Bradley says.

"Sure. Very few of my escorts use their real names. It's a safeguard, if you know what I mean."

"How do you report their income?" Kenne asks.

"I use the information they give me on their applications."

"Are they on payroll?"

Kerrigan laughs and says, "Independent contractors."

Kenne shakes his head and hands Kerrigan his business card and says, "Please contact me if you think of anything else."

"Oh, one other thing. She used to have a motto that she'd tell all of her companions. 'If anyone asks where you were, just tell them you went fishing and caught a beautiful trout'."

Chapter Sixteen

Back at Headquarters

The next morning Kenne is sitting in his office preparing for the noon media conference he has scheduled. Sam knocks on the open door and walks in.

"I've got the information you wanted on the dead guy and Poe's girlfriend," He tells Kenne.

"Leave the reports on the desk. I'll get to them in a bit," Kenne says.

Sam sets the reports on the desk, leaves the office and Kenne gets back to his conference preparation. Ten minutes later he picks up Sam's report on Victor De La Hoz and reads it.

De La Hoz had a life of crime since he was fourteen. It started out with petty crimes as a teenage gang member and escalated to breaking and entering, armed robbery, drug possession and distribution and assault. His mother was a prostitute and he did some pimping for her.

He served eight years in Lompoc and had various cellmates including Jason Poe. He was a trouble maker and once assaulted a guard which got him some time in solitary. He supposedly found God while in solitary and became a born again Christian. He started studying theology to mend his ways. The parole board bought it and he was paroled early.

After his release he had financial troubles and moved in with Poe for a short time. While living with Poe he took software courses online to learn a new trade as a software technician. He graduated from the course and got a job as an assistant software technician with an insurance company. That job only lasted a short time. He held a couple of other short-term positions after that. His supervisors knew nothing about his personal life. He died fourteen months ago of a drug overdose.

Kenne looks at the report for a moment, sets it down and picks up the Ana Trout report and reads it.

Sam couldn't find anything of her existence before her arrest for solicitation. She served two years in the Central California Women's Facility at Chowchilla for assault. She assaulted one of her potential tricks, an undercover cop, who tried to arrest her.

Sam checked it all for identification. There was no local birth certificate, California driver's license and no marriage license under the name Ana Trout. Yet her name came up on Sam's social security list.

Sam checked it out with the California Franchise Tax Board and the only records they had on her was tax documents filed in prior years but no tax returns. Sam checked with the Internal Revenue Service and received the same information.

Kenne sits back in his chair and rubs his chin and thinks to himself that Barbara Kerrigan said all her escorts use aliases. Kenne opens Trout's folder holding her yellow sheet and starts to insert Sam's report into the folder when he stops. He focuses on Ana Trout's social security number on the yellow sheet and realizes something is wrong. He's seen that number before. Where has he seen it?

After thinking for a moment he scrambles to find Jason Poe's file folder. It was lying on the corner of his desk under other paper work. He opens the folder and picks up Poe's yellow sheet. He looks at the social security number and compares it to Trout's. They are the same. The social security number on both yellow sheets is 533-11-6646.

Kenne takes the two yellow sheets and rushes to the 'Line of Play' dominoes table. The first nine numbers of the dominoes are 5-3-3-1-1-6-6-4-6.

Detective McDonald is sitting at her desk near Kenne.

Kenne calls her, "Mac, come here, quick."

Mac rushes to Kenne's side and he hands her the two yellow sheets.

"Study these very carefully and tell me what information you see that is the same," Kenne instructs.

Mac studies the two forms for a minute and shakes her head a couple of times.

"Look at the socials," Kenne hints.

Mac does so and then shouts, "Holy shit!"

Now compare the socials to the first nine numbers on the dominoes. She does so.

"Holy shit!" she shouts again.

By this time everyone in the squad room has gathered around the two of them.

"What in hell have we got here?" Mac asks.

"I don't know yet," Kenne answers.

Bradley leans in and asks, "What's going on?"

"Get Poe and take him to number one. Don't bother to contact his lawyer," Kenne says without answering the question.

****

Poe and Bradley are sitting at the interrogation table when Kenne enters the room. He sits down and sets three file folders on the table in front of him.

"What's going on here?" Poe asks, "Haven't I been through enough?"

"Just shut up," Kenne says in a mean tone. "This isn't a question and answer session. I need to get some information from you. And I mean now."

Poe, who is handcuffed sets his hands on the table and asks, "What kind of information?"

"Let's start with your ex-cellmate Victor. Tell me everything you know about him."

Poe looks at Kenne and thinks for a moment. He glances over at Bradley and he nods his head at Poe.

"We were cellmates for about two years on my first trip to Lompoc except for the sixty days he spent in solitary for hitting that guard. The bastard deserved it. After solitary he started preaching Jesus to me. I made out like I cared because I didn't want to get him mad. He had a real bad temper.

"I was released on parole shortly after that. Not long after that he got out on parole and we ran into each other at one of my old haunts that I had told him about. He was having money problems. Couldn't get a job. I talked my brother into letting him move in with us."

"Did he have access to the computer?" Kenne asks.

"I was just going to get to that. He started taking a course on the internet. I'm not sure what it was all about but it helped him get a job. When my brother moved to Colorado we had to all split up because we couldn't afford the rent.

"I heard shortly after that he died from a drug overdose. It didn't figure. When he became a born again Christian he was off the stuff."

"Anything else?" Kenne asks.

"No. That's about it."

"Tell me about your relationship with Ana Trout," Kenne continues.

"Stormy," he says and then laughs silently to himself.

"Start at the beginning when you first met her."

"Like I said before, I met her through her friend Asia. Shortly after that she moved in with me. She was a moody person. One day she was fun and jovial and the next day moody and cranky. In fact, at times she acted as if she didn't know who I was. Then one day we had a fight and I hit her. I hit her pretty hard. She reported domestic abuse and I got two years in Lompoc.

"When I got out I looked up Asia. She was working at one of those topless clubs on Highland.

"The Dreamgirls Club," Bradley interrupts.

"Yeah, that was it. She told me Ana had moved back in with her. I apologized to Ana for my past behavior and we got back together again, moving in with my brother. We had the same problems and one day I slapped her. The next day she was gone and I never saw her again."

"We've done some legwork and have some information on Ana," Kenne informs Poe. "Did you know how she made her living?"

"Yes. But I didn't care."

"Did you notice anything strange about her besides the mood swings and her not knowing you when she was in one of those moods?"

"No. Nothing that I can think of."

"Was she home alone at any time?"

"Yeah. During the day except maybe when Victor was around. She worked nights."

"Then she had access to the computer."

"Yeah. I guess so. But I never saw her use it. I didn't think she knew much about it."

"We know that she attended the July fourth party at Dobbs Construction with you. Did she ever leave your side when you were there?"

"Maybe once or twice. You know, to use the facilities."

"Have you ever known her to take or be in possession of drugs or smoke marijuana?"

"Not that I know of."

"Did you know that Ana Trout wasn't her real name?"

"It wasn't?"

"We're having trouble identifying her. Did she have any birthmarks, scars or tattoos on her body?"

"No."

Poe looks Kenne in the eyes and asks, "What's this all about? What's Ana and Victor got to do with this?"

Kenne leaves the room without answering Poe.

****

As Kenne enters the squad room he asks Lamar to step into his office. Kenne sits on the corner of his desk while Lamar stands near the doorway.

"I want you and Trop to go to Victor De La Hoz' last place of residence and interview the manager," Kenne instructs him. "I'm interested in one thing. Did he ever have any women guests and if so, get a description?"

"That's it?" Lamar questions Kenne.

"That's it."

On his way out of the office, Lamar runs into Bradley and says to him, "I think the boss has lost it. He wants me and Trop to do some legwork on a dead man."

Bradley looks at him and says, "Don't you know, that's part of your indoctrination."

Lamar shakes his head and walks away muttering to his self, "Big joke."

Bradley smiles and heads toward Kenne's office. Kenne is still sitting on the corner of his desk looking at his notes that he's going to use for the press conference when Bradley enters the office.

"Lieutenant, are you thinking what I think you're thinking?" Bradley asks.

"And what's that?"

"That this Ana Trout babe is our serial killer."

Kenne gives him some philosophy, "A professor of criminal science once told me, 'suspect everyone and leave no stone unturned'."

****

Once again, the conference room is standing room only as reporters from all media venues are in attendance. Kenne enters the room and steps in front of the podium which is lined with microphones. Captain Manning, Sergeant Singleton and Detective

Bradley enter after Kenne and stand behind him.

Kenne takes a moment to look around the room and then starts the news conference, "I'm going to give you some information and after that I will take questions.

"First, let me apologize for being so abrupt with you at the last news conference but the Los Angeles County Sheriff's Department's priority is to capture and provide evidence to the District Attorney's office on a suspect in every case. No exceptions. And then, and only then, inform the media of that event. I know you want to sell newspapers and inform the general public through the visual media about important events and we understand that but as I said, we do have our priorities.

"The information I have for you today is still preliminary but we do have some new developments in the Domino serial murder case. We have a person of interest in custody and are concentrating our investigation on whether that person is the domino killer or is linked in some way. We are also attempting to link yesterday's event in Glendale to the domino killer."

A buzz runs through the event as news people start talking to each other.

Kenne continues, "We believe that the event was not an act of terrorism and have our suspicions that Domino may be involved. We are working diligently to determine whether this is in fact a possibility. We ask that you be patient while we check out all avenues leading up to the Glendale event. We will inform you of the progress of the investigation when we have some concrete information. Now I'll take questions in an orderly fashion with one question per person. Please raise your hand and I'll point to you."

Kenne points to Deborah Tyler of KABC News who is sitting in the front row.

Deborah stands up and asks, "Can you release the identity of the person of interest you have in custody?"

"Come on Deborah, you know that's not within the bounds of our protocol," Kenne answers.

He points to Arthur Gibbons of KCBS News.

Gibbons stands up and asks, "What makes you think the domino killer is responsible for yesterday's tragedy?"

"Like I said, at the present time we are checking this out. Our main concern is that we need to investigate all violent events of any kind as possibility being performed by the same perpetrator."

Kenne points to Felicia Hammond of KNBC News

She stands up and asks, "If you have a person of interest in custody, how can you link yesterday's tragedy to him?"

"According to Glendale Fire Chief Sparks, the bomb was ignited by a timing device. Which means the bomb could have been set in place long before it exploded."

He points to Luis Garcia, crime journalist for the Los Angeles Times.

Garcia remains seated and says, "There were ten fatalities, three still in serious condition and nineteen injured yesterday in Glendale. Don't you think enough is enough?"

Kenne says, "I agree with you one-hundred percent, Luis. I want to thank you all for coming and further information will be released through the Sheriff's Department media services."

Kenne walks away from the podium and exits the room followed by Manning, Singleton and Bradley.

In the hallway on the walk to the rear elevators, Manning says, "I don't think you gave them everything they wanted to hear."

"I gave them everything I wanted them and Domino to hear."

"I thought you have Domino in custody?" Manning asks.

Kenne responds, "Do I?"

****

When Kenne enters the squad room, Sam motions for him to come over to his desk.

"I've finished background checks on all the 6-2-2-0 residents. Everybody's clean except for a few traffic and parking tickets," Sam says.

Kenne says, "Thank you. I'm not surprised."

Later that afternoon Dr. Goldstein pays Kenne a visit.

"What brings you here, Marv?" Kenne asks as he greets him.

Goldstein pulls up a chair and answers, "I'm here to get an update on your nemesis, Domino."

"Nemesis. That's an appropriate characterization."

"I saw your press conference. You looked old and tired on live TV."

"I love you, too," Kenne responds.

"What happened yesterday in Glendale was not the normal actions of a serial killer," Goldstein states.

Kenne shows him the note along with the domino. Goldstein reads the note, looks at the domino and shakes his head.

After a moment of thought he says, "It doesn't make any sense unless he's trying to show us his versatility using different murder instruments for each crime."

"That's my thinking, too," Kenne says. "I do have a question for you but I want you to think about your answer before you give me a response. Could Domino be a female?"

Goldstein looks at Kenne and squints. Then he rubs his forehead for about thirty seconds and looks at Kenne again.

"I'd have to say highly unlikely …. But possible? … Maybe," Goldstein says hesitantly.

"In this case, I'm not leaving any possibility out."

"What makes you think it might be a woman?" Goldstein asks.

"The pieces are falling together just like the dominoes. I just have a gut feeling about this."

"It wouldn't be the first time for a female serial killer," Goldstein comments. "I believe, if I recollect correctly, there's been ten of them in U. S. history. If you think it's a woman, do you have any idea who she is?"

"Yes and no," Kenne answers.

The two men look at each other for a long moment and then laugh at the same time.

"It's no laughing matter but I just couldn't help it. It makes no sense to me," Goldstein says.

"I know. Me neither."

Goldstein rises from his seat and tells Kenne as he heads toward the door, "Keep me in the loop. You've definitely got my attention."

Chapter Seventeen

The Numbers Simplified

Kenne Narration: "One definition of stress is 'a state of mental or emotional strain or tension resulting from adverse or very demanding circumstances'. That's a perfect description of how I'm feeling right now. I figured sitting here in the Westwood Sports Lounge drinking a few beers during Happy Hour is a good start of combating my stress. Before I came here I made two phone calls. The first was to FBI agent Parker Cunningham. I asked him to track down Ana Trout. I gave him all the information that I have. The second phone call was to Giana. I asked her to meet me here. I am waiting for her arrival."

Kenne is sitting at a small round table on a bar stool in the middle of the lounge's bar area. Giana enters the lounge and sits down on a bar stool opposite Kenne. Preoccupied with his stress, he doesn't notice her entrance until she sits down. He looks at her and smiles.

"You look terrific," he states.

"I know," she proudly answers.

Kenne waves for the bar maid to bring two beers for Giana and then moves his stool next to her.

"You look exhausted," Giana says.

"I feel exhausted," Kenne confirms her observation.

"I should probably take you home and put you to bed," Giana quips.

"What a marvelous idea," Kenne says with a big grin on his face.

They lean toward each other and kiss.

Giana drank her two beers while Kenne finished his first happy hour order of two beers and ordered and drank two more while they were watching a Dodgers' baseball game on a large screen television. He had walked over from the office so he was without wheels, which was a good thing. Giana had driven over and was still sober enough to drive. She drove them back to her place and before they got out of the car they held a necking session for about ten minutes.

"Let's go inside," Giana suggests.

Without saying a word, Kenne exits the car and Giana slides over and exits on his side, also. Once inside the building Kenne stops and turns toward Giana.

"I've got a question for you. When I called the other day, someone whose voice sounded like yours answered the phone. She was rather rude and said I had the wrong number."

"Oh, that was probably my sister. She stays with me when she's in town. She travels a lot. Her job. You never know when she's going to show up. She never calls. Just appears."

Once inside Giana's apartment it took them about thirty seconds to undress and jump into bed. They make love twice and Kenne spent the night. They make love in the morning again and jump in the shower together before breakfast.

Giana serves him scrambled eggs, bacon, rye toast with jam and coffee for breakfast. Hungry as a bear, Kenne eats as if it was a gourmet meal. After breakfast Giana offers to drive him to the office but he refuses. Instead, he calls Lamar for a ride.

While waiting for Lamar, Kenne and Giana have their first real conversation while sitting at the table.

"You look a lot better than you did last night," Giana says.

"I feel better. Don't know if it was the sex or the food?"

"I think it was just the fact that you were able to get your mind off of that case you're working on."

"What do you know about that?"

"Just what I've seen on television."

"When this is over, how about you and me taking a trip together, if it doesn't interfere with your work schedule?" Kenne asks.

"Where?" she answers with a question of her own.

"I don't know. Hawaii, Tahiti, Palm Springs. Where would you like to go?"

"Let me think about it for a day or so."

Changing the subject, Kenne asks, "By the way, where do you work?"

"I'm currently unemployed."

"What do you do when you do work?"

"I'm a flutist."

Surprised by the answer, Kenne asks, "You're a what?"

"A flutist. I play the flute. Like in music," she proudly answers.

"What does your sister do that she's away all the time?"

"Why all the questions?" Giana asks.

"I guess it's just the cop in me."

Giana gets up, sits on Kenne's lap and kisses him.

"I like the cop in me," she whispers in his ear.

"You are very nasty," Kenne says in a jovial tone as he slaps her in the butt.

A car horn sounds from the street below. Kenne nudges Giana off his lap and looks out the window. Lamar has arrived with Kenne's ride to the office.

"I've got to go," he says while heading to the door. "I'll see you tonight, if that's okay with you?"

"I'm looking forward to it," she says with a smirk on her face. "She's a flight attendant."

Kenne looks back at her and asks, "Who's a flight attendant?"

"My sister. She's a flight attendant."

"What airline?"

"I'm really not sure. I don't pay much attention to her life. Besides, does it matter?"

"Not really," Kenne answers as he closes the door behind him.

****

On the drive to the office Lamar fills Kenne in on his findings from his visit to Victor's former residence.

"His landlady said she knows of only one woman that visited him. She stayed overnight a couple of times. She described her as an attractive brunette in her late twenty's or early thirties. Her hair was down to her shoulders and she was always well-dressed, about five-five to five-six with voluptuous breasts."

"She said voluptuous?" Kenne asks.

"Not exactly. She said healthy breasts. I replaced it with voluptuous. It sounds better to me."

Kenne looks at Lamar for a few seconds and then informs him, "You need to find yourself a girl friend."

Lamar grins at him and says, "I went out on a date last month."

Changing the subject Kenne states, "The description fits Ana Trout. Whoever and wherever the hell she is."

Lamar nods his head in agreement and says, "We'll find her."

****

There was a fair amount of street traffic for a Thursday morning which made the ride to the office long and boring. In fact, Lamar wanted to use his siren and flashing lights to circumvent the problem but Kenne wouldn't let him. While they were stuck in traffic, Kenne called the office and asked Sergeant Singleton to notify everyone in the squad that he wanted to hold a meeting as soon as he got in. He also asked him to invite Captain Manning.

The squad members are standing around taking a coffee break when Kenne and Lamar arrive. Kenne has them gather around the 'Line of Play' table and notices that Captain Manning is nowhere in sight.

"Where's the captain?" Kenne asks Detective McDonald.

"He got called to a meeting at Sheriff Unger's office," she answers.

"Okay, let's get started without him. We now know that the first nine numbers relates to a social security number that belongs to Jason Poe. We also know that Ana Trout has been using that same social security number. Therefore, we need to take those first nine numbers out of the equation and focus on the other numbers. 6-6-2-2-0-0-4. Since the nine social security numbers are in the same order as the domino numbers here, let's assume the answer to the riddle of these other numbers are also in sequence. Any ideas?"

"A phone number without an area code," Mac suggests.

Kenne looks at Sam and tells him, "Check it out."

Sam rushes to his computer and goes to work.

"Ana's description and yellow sheet says she's five-foot six-inches tall. That's sixty-six inches," Bradley reminds everyone.

"Okay. Let's assume the six-six domino is a clue to her height," Kenne says. "But let's not take the six-six numbers out of the equation just yet."

Ramirez quips, "If the six-six is her height in inches, I'll bet the rest of the numbers isn't her weight."

"Let's stay focused, here. Try to put the humor on a back burner," Kenne states gruffly.

"Sorry," Ramirez says in an apologetic tone.

"Maybe it's a zip code," David suggests.

"Sam. Check out zip code 22004 on the internet and see what you come with," Kenne says.

Sam takes about thirty seconds and gives everyone the answer, "It's not a zip code but a postal code for some place in Guatemala with the unusual name Agua Blanca Deto De Jutiapa."

"Sounds like a thriving metropolis to me," Ramirez remarks.

Kenne looks at him with daggers in his eyes. Ramirez holds up his right hand and mouths that he's sorry.

"That postal code makes no sense to me," Kenne says. "Anybody have any ideas? Sam, jumble the numbers and see what you come up with."

Mac hands Kenne Poe's yellow sheet and points to his first booking identification number under his mug shot. The number is 6622004.

"Mac, check out who might have access to that information," Kenne orders.

"Why check?" she states. "How about someone identifying him from a mug shot in a domestic abuse case."

"Ana Trout," Kenne states.

"Or his first wife," Bradley suggests.

"No. I've checked her out. She's remarried with two kids and lives in Syracuse, New York. She moved there six years ago."

Kenne pauses for a moment and states, "that booking number 6-6-2-2-0-0-4 just might be an important clue. Then again it just might be leading us up a blind alley."

Kenne stops for a moment and a surprised look appears on his face. The word alley strikes a chord. He excuses himself leaving Sergeant Singleton in charge.

****

From his office, Kenne uses his cell phone to call Alicia on hers. When she answers she is excited to hear his voice. After some small talk about how each of them are, Kenne gets to the main reason for the call.

"I have a question to ask you," Kenne says. "It's about that shadowy figure you saw in the alley."

"Is that why you called?" she shouts.

"It's one of the reasons. After all you are my star witness."

"I'm your only witness and it's the only reason. I should hang up."

"It's not the only reason but it's an important one. I need your help," Kenne pleads.

"Okay. What is it?" she concedes but in a reluctant tone of voice.

"That shadowy figure you saw in the alley. Could it have been a woman? Maybe her hips were swinging as she walked. Or some other tell tale sign."

After thinking back for a moment she tells Kenne, "Come to think of it his ... or should I say her hips were swaying a bit like a woman. Is that important?"

"Yes," he answers. "Very important."

"You mean the domino killer is a woman?"

"It's possible but please keep this confidential. I don't want my suspicions to get out just yet."

"I won't say a word. I promise."

Changing the subject, Kenne asks, "Can I see you again?"

Alicia stays silent.

Kenne asks, "Did you hear me?"

"I heard you," she answers. "I guess I'd like that. But not for awhile"

"I'll call you just as soon as this Domino thing comes to a finish. We'll talk."

"We'll do more than that," she states just before hanging up.

Just as Kenne sets his cell phone on his desk it rings. He looks at the caller's number and identifies it as FBI agent Cunningham calling. He answers the phone and talks to Cunningham for about ten minutes. Cunningham's call was in answer to Kenne's request about helping him find Ana Trout.

Chapter Eighteen

A Woman or a Smoke Screen

The squad is discussing possible scenarios for the 6-6-2-2-0-0-4 numbers when Kenne joins them.

"Listen up," Kenne says. "I've just spoken to FBI agent Cunningham and he's given me some information on Ana Trout dating back a couple of years. It seems she traveled to Atlanta on a Delta Airlines red-eye flight two years ago on Friday, August 29th, the Labor Day weekend. She used Victor De La Hoz' debit card to pay for the one-way ticket. On arrival in Atlanta she rented a car using the same debit card. The car was never returned on the due date. However, it was found abandoned about two weeks later in a parking garage in Greenville, South Carolina. From all indications it looks like Ana Trout disappeared at that date in time in Greenville. Or at least the person using that alias."

"Lieutenant," David interrupts. "We've been discussing those numbers and we've come up with some ideas."

"Let it wait," Kenne states. "I've got some ideas of my own. Ana Trout, or whatever her real name is planned this rampage two years ago because she was mad at Poe for the first domestic abuse attack on her for which he went to jail. I mean, she was really pissed off. Her plan was to frame him for a serial crime because of his past abuse history. Somehow she ran across the domino serial killing spree of six decades ago. How unique she decided and proceeded with her plot to frame Poe after he was released from jail.

"In order to accomplish a perfect frame she decided that she needed to take a trip back east and get all the information possible on the domino killer of the fifties. In fact, she actually expanded on that whole scenario with an ingenious plot that would both confuse us and lead us to Poe.

"Joshua, if you remember, Victor De La Hoz took up computer software classes on the internet. During his internet activities he discovered the strange information that Trout left behind to help frame Poe. He put it all together and was blackmailing Trout in a way. That blackmail wasn't about money. It was about sexual favors. Trout killed De La Hoz by administering a drug overdose and then used his debit card for her trip back east.

"She used the sick mother excuse with her employer and friends to return to Atlanta and Greenville to learn more about Hall's crime spree. She then abandoned the Ana

Trout identity and returned to Los Angeles to put her plan in motion. After Poe was released from jail she met up with him through his obsession of hanging out in topless clubs. She made it look like a surprise happenstance. But, it was perfectly planned like everything else.

"After another abuse by Poe, which Trout proffered, they broke up. However, Trout now knew where Poe lived and worked and used that information to follow him and commit the murders when she knew he couldn't come up with a substantiated alibi. The major question that is haunting me is why she selected such an elaborate and ingenious plan including using dominoes as clues to lead us to the serial killer's identity."

"It's my opinion that it would take a genius to invent a plot like this," Trop states.

"Exactly," Kenne responds.

All the squad members shake their head in disbelief.

"Now here's another scenario," Kenne states. "What if Poe is the domino killer and is framing Trout for the murders?"

"What?" the entire squad says, simultaneously.

"Let me run this by you," Kenne says starting with his alternate scenario. "Let's suppose Poe elaborated this crime scenario to frame Ana Trout. Why? Because she turned him in on the first domestic violence charges and he was mad as hell. He was the one that used his computer to plant the information for his revenge plot. He killed De La Hoz for two reasons. He was having an affair with Ana and he needed his debit card. He had found out about Trout's planned trip to Atlanta from De La Hoz and decided to kill her, too. That's why she disappeared. He then masqueraded as Trout to Atlanta on the Labor Day weekend to give him an extra day to research the fifties domino killings. He used Trout's ID's for his flight and car rental identity.

"He arrived in Atlanta early on Saturday morning. Probably slept on the plane. He rented a car and then went to the Atlanta Journal Constitution library and researched the domino killings there. Later that day or early Sunday he drove to Greenville. It's about a hundred mile trip. He did his research there and then flew home from Greenville on Monday using cash to pay for the flight. Before leaving Greenville, he destroyed all of Trout's forged identity documents thus making her disappear. He was back in time to report for work on Tuesday.

"Two things are a bit confusing using this scenario. The first is the time line involving the matching social security numbers. If Poe is the guilty party, when did he forge her social security card and driver's license because the date on her yellow sheet is while Poe is serving his second term in Lompoc? Which means he would have had to replace the identification documents before his conviction. It doesn't make sense.

"The second thing that bothers me about this scenario is what really did happen to Ana Trout? Did he kill her? So, it makes more sense that Trout is still alive and she is our serial killer because she could have forged her driver's license and the numbers on her social security card at any time."

"What a mess," Mac states shaking her head.

"Not a mess," Kenne informs her. "Ingenious. That's why I think Poe is being framed. As I said before he just isn't smart enough to pull this off.

"Let's take some time to digest this information. We'll meet at noon tomorrow to give us a better perspective. Lamar, you're in charge of lunch."

Lamar shakes his head in response as if to say 'why me'.

****

After spending another night with Giana, at her place, Kenne meets with Dr. Goldstein and Harley regarding the mindset of past female serial killers. Before he left the office the previous evening he had asked Sam to run a list of female serial killers from the internet. Sam's report is sitting on his desk upon Kenne's arrival.

Kenne opens the meeting, "I'm of the belief that Domino is a female. We don't know where or who she is. She masqueraded as Ana Trout for a number of years. That's not her real name. The only information we have on her is a yellow sheet with a picture that's four-years-old.

"The mug shot on the yellow sheet probably doesn't do her justice. No makeup and unruly blonde hair distorts her normal appearance and makes her look much older than she is. Her current hair color is not blonde, but brunette. It's probably her natural color. I've got our artists working on possible images of how she might look today as a brunette with different makeup applications.

"The reason I've asked the two of you here is to go over the profiles of past female serial killers to see if we can spot some similarities that they have in common with Domino. Oh, by the way Marv, you were right about there being ten of them."

"Most serial killers are men in their twenties or thirties," Goldstein informs the group. "They usually come from lower-to-middle class backgrounds. Yes, there have been ten infamous female serial killers throughout our history. I've never had an occasion to do a study on them so it will be interesting to see if we can come up with something in common."

"Okay, let's get started," Kenne says as he turns on his recording device. "Most of the women who committed serial crimes did so in the 1890's and early 1900's. So we're dealing with a different time period but I believe they all have one thing in common. They are all mentally deranged.

"Lavinia Fisher is the first on record. She was active along with her husband in the early 1800's. They ran a boarding house in South Carolina. Rumors were that she would poison male guests to make them sick and unable to defend themselves and her husband would finish the job. They did it for monetary reasons only as they would confiscate their victim's cash and goods.

"Anybody see any similarities with Trout's rampage?" Kenne asks.

"Nothing," says Goldstein. "Outside of the fact that the original domino killer started his spree in South Carolina. But he wasn't a female."

"How about you, Harley?" Kenne asks.

Harley shakes his head and says, "I don't see anything."

"Let's move on to Aileen Wuornos," Kenne continues. "She had a rotten child-hood. Was assaulted and raped at thirteen and became a prostitute. She murdered seven of her johns in Florida."

"Hollywood made a movie about her," Harley interjects.

"That's right," Goldstein agrees. "I saw that movie. The actress that played Wuornos went through the whole movie without makeup. It greatly altered her normal looks with makeup."

"Similar to Trout's mug shot and her everyday looks?" Kenne asks.

"Yes, definitely," Goldstein answers.

"If Ana is a copycat of the domino killer of the fifties, why not make her appearance be a copycat of another serial killer," Harley states.

"Good point," Kenne observes. "We also know that Trout comes from a mysterious background. Don't know about her childhood but I'd guess it was rotten just like Wuornos'. She was a topless dancer for awhile then graduated into bigger things. Worked as an escort and more than likely earned money on the side supplying extra-curricular personal services."

"You mean she was a whore," Harley says with a grin on his face.

"We can use that description of her if it makes you more comfortable," Kenne says, raising his eyebrows. "Let's not forget she served time in jail for assault on one of her escort customers who was a cop.

"Belle Gunness was another of the early serial killers. She was born in Norway in 1889 and emigrated here, settling in Chicago. Like Fisher, she kept her serial killing close to home. Her husband and children died of mysterious causes. Also other rich suitors. She was a brutal person but men were drawn to her charms. After a mysterious fire in her home she disappeared never to be found.

"Trout seems to draw men with her charms. And that disappearing thing matches Belle. Only one thing. Trout seems to have disappeared before her crimes, not after."

"There's nothing there," Goldstein says.

"Our next beauty is Jane Toppan," Kenne continues. "She was active between 1885 and the early 1900's. She was a nurse and experimented with patients using a combination of medicines and chemicals to tweak their nervous systems. She committed other murders later on and while in custody confessed to dozens of murders. She admitted to being aroused by the process of killing. She was declared insane."

"That's nice to know that we had an exceptional legal system back then," Harley states.

"Trout may be aroused by the killings," Goldstein says. "It might even give her a sexual release of some sorts. But deep down she wants to be caught. That's why the dominoes are left as clues. Puzzling clues, but clues. So far you've done a good job but there is still a lot of work to be done and it won't be easy."

"Did you know that Velma Barfield was a slacker when it came to serial killing?" Kenne says. "She only killed five people. She also kept her mayhem close to home killing a boyfriend and her mother. After her conviction she became a devout Christian before her execution in 1977. The only connection that Trout has to Barfield is that we suppose De La Hoz was trying to convert her. Not sure if he did."

"Probably nothing there," Goldstein interjects. "Continue."

"Next on my list is Amelia Dyer. She's another nineteenth century killer and probably the most infamous of all time – at least in my mind. She killed hundreds of victims. The really gruesome part is they were infants. She was a baby trafficker and those that weren't trafficked died of neglect and starvation."

"Trout has absolutely zero in common with that monster," Harley says.

"Nannie Doss is another one who kept her killing close to home. She murdered four husbands and a boatload of other relatives including her sisters, her mother and two of her kids. She was finally caught when she tried killing her fifth husband. Once again, I can't see Trout having anything in common with Nannie.

"Interesting name," Harley interjects. "I must remind my wife to never hire one for my kids."

Kenne and Goldstein look at each other shake their heads and laugh.

"Bertha Gifford and Jeanne Weber were two more members of the fair sex who were active at the turn of the century. Bertha used arsenic to kill about two dozen. Jeanne was another one who chose family members to kill. She started by murdering her sister's children and sometime later had a hand in killing her own child. Authorities weren't sure how many others.

"The last one is Dorothea Puente. She was active in the 1980's. Her motives were strictly monetary. If you remember she's a California girl who owned a boarding house in Sacramento. She would receive all mail delivered and was most interested in her boarders benefit checks. She would cash the checks and then eventually kill the boarder. When she was caught she tried to convince everyone that they all died of natural causes."

"Every one of those women had different motives for their killing sprees," Goldstein advises. "One thing we know is that all serial killers, whether male or female, are mentally deranged and they don't follow any consistent pattern. Ana Trout has conceived a new serial killing concept by playing a game with the authorities and she's probably enjoying it more than we despise it. There is one thing that she has that no other serial killer had."

"What's that?" Kenne asks.

"An incredible imagination," Goldstein responds. "Actually, she has the imagination of a genius with a very high I.Q and is probably the most unique serial killer in history.

"And more brutal. She doesn't use poison like most of the women before her and she doesn't know her victims as she picks them at random."

"Here's an idea that just popped into my head," Harley exclaims. "Could Ana be a relative of Albert Hill – like a granddaughter - and she's finishing what he started? Like I've said before, she's created a new sport. Playing with our minds while she kills people on a whim using different deadly weapons."

"Your idea of a distant relative of Hill has crossed my mind," Kenne answers Harley's question. "I've even asked the FBI to do a profile on Hill and they've come up with nothing. No female companions, living or dead."

Goldstein offers his experience on the subject," More than ninety-nine percent of the male population throughout history has had some sort of relationship with the opposite sex. It's entirely possible that Hill had a secret lover that nobody knew about. It's possible she had a child and her child had a child. Therefore, we could be dealing with a third generation relative of Hill's, like a granddaughter."

Harley asks, "If that's the case, why here? Why not Atlanta or Greenville?"

"Because she lives here," Kenne answers. "As soon as I have our artist's likenesses, we'll see if Poe or any of her past acquaintances will recognize her. We'll also splatter her face all over the news as a person of interest in the domino slayings. If we're lucky, someone will recognize her."

Chapter Nineteen

Sketchy I. D.

Kenne Narration: "I had asked Giana about taking the weekend in Palm Springs. I wanted to get away and take some time to clear my head. I've always thought better about a case when taking some time away from it. She said the timing wasn't good. She had a previous commitment. I was distraught over her decision but decided to accept the idea of spending the weekend at the office and contemplating Domino's next move. I was sure she would launch another episode, soon. In fact, the zero/four domino had me thinking Saturday, which was four days after the Glendale bombing, was the exact time period. I was sure the zero/four sided domino also gave me the clue as to where or what time. I had alerted my squad as to my thinking and they were all on alert. I spent the night trying to figure something out. Even put myself in her place in deciding what the zero/four meant."

Kenne woke up startled from a bad dream. It was a little after six in the morning and it was time to rise anyways after spending the night on the uncomfortable cot stored it the supply room next to his office. Kenne has always had trouble remembering his dreams, specially the bizarre ones, but the one that woke him up was haunting him while taking a shower in the locker room on the second floor rear of the building.

Upon returning to his office he noticed he had left the fifty-inch television mounted on the wall opposite his desk running all night. However, the cable box sitting on the credenza below the television was shut down. He had the system installed for nights like this to keep him company. He reached for the remote to turn the television off but stopped and had an alarming look on his face.

Last night before trading his chair for the uncomfortable cot he was dozing off to a movie that was playing. The movie was The Ten Commandments with Charleston Heston. The last thing he remembered about the movie was when God was burning the commandments into the sacred tablets. Then he remembered that's what his dream was about.

He rushed over to Sam's computer and logged into the internet. Once there he typed the words 'The Fourth Commandment' into the open space for input. The information came up and Kenne read it.

"Remember the Sabbath day, to keep it holy. Six days you shall labor and do all your work, but the seventh day is the Sabbath of the Lord your God. In it you shall do no work: you, nor your son, nor your daughter, nor your male servant, nor your female servant, nor your cattle, nor your stranger who is within your gates. For in six days the Lord made the heavens and the earth, the sea, and all that is in them, and rested the seventh day. Therefore the Lord blessed the Sabbath day and hallowed it." Exodus 20:8-11

Kenne read the commandment over and over again trying to understand the meaning of the commandment in relation to Domino. After a bit, he grabbed his calendar that had the days and dates of Domino's slaying and none of them were performed on Sunday. He thought to himself that De La Hoz must have converted her to Christianity before she killed him. Kenne kept reading more information about The Fourth Commandment.

Of the ten, this is the only commandment God specifically commanded man to remember! Before Moses brought those holy, sacred tables containing the very hand-writing of God down from the burning mountain top, God said, Surely My Sabbaths you shall keep, for it is a sign between Me and you throughout your generations, that you may know that I am the Lord who sanctifies you" (Exodus 31:13).

In this fourth precept the Sabbath is not introduced as a new institution but as having been founded at creation. It is to be remembered and observed as the memorial of the Creator's work. Pointing to God as the Maker of the heavens and the earth, it distinguishes the true God from all false gods. All who keep the seventh day signify by this act that they are worshipers of the only true God, the God who created and the God who longs to recreate them in His righteousness. Thus the Sabbath is the sign of man's allegiance to God as long as there are any upon the earth to serve Him. And it is also our weekly reminder of God's pledge to deliver us from bondage of sin, to recreate is in His image.

Kenne didn't have a clue what those last two paragraphs meant but he figured they must be important. He kept reading.

The fourth commandment is the only one of all the ten in which are found both the name and title of the Lawgiver. Without this commandment there is no hint as to who wrote the law or why we should listen to or obey its claims. It is the only one that shows by whose authority the law was given. In this sense it contains the seal of God, affixed to His law as evidence of its authenticity and binding force. God asks us to remember the Sabbath, the seventh day of the week, which He blessed, hallowed and sanctified. He longs to have a holy people that will serve Him because they love Him. He set aside one day, the seventh day each week, as holy time when he could enjoy a special time of fellowship with our Creator. Only His presence in our lives brings holiness. Those who worship God on His holy day – who worship Him in "spirit and in truth" – are showing by worshipping on the seventh day Sabbath in obedience to His command that they, through His power, are obedient to His commands every day. They are not just "seventh day Christians," but they are "seven day Christians" – God is their God, their Ruler, their Salvation, their Redeemer and their Sanctifier every day of the week.

After giving it some thought, Kenne realizes what the four side of the domino means. He prints the information and makes copies for everyone in the squad.

The squad members start arriving around eight o'clock and shortly after that the artist delivers his sketches of Ana Trout to Kenne. He calls Lamar and Bradley into his office and instructs them to show Poe the sketches and then make plans to show them to the topless managers, Barbara at the escort service and Ana's ex-roommate Asia Fantasia. Lamar and Bradley leave his office with copies of the sketches and Bradley has a smile on his face knowing he's going to get a first row seat at the topless club, once again.

Meanwhile, Kenne asks the rest of the squad members into his office and distributes a printed copy of The Fourth Commandment to all of them.

"Read this," he instructs the group.

They all take about five minutes to read the information and have puzzled looks on their faces.

"What's this all about?" Trop asks.

"It's about the four on the last domino. It's about Domino's next victim," Kenne informs the squad. "Have any of you noticed that Domino has never worked on Sunday? She takes the Sabbath seriously. So seriously that her next victim is going to be a Seventh Day Adventist Minister today at four o'clock. Well, not necessarily at four but today for sure."

"That's the day that they worship," Sam says with confidence.

"Exactly," Kenne agrees.

"How in the world did you come up with this allegory?" Mac asks.

254

"You wouldn't believe me, if I told you. Here's what I want you all to do. Sam, print a list of all Seventh Day Adventist Churches in the county from the internet. I want addresses and phone numbers. Then all of you will divide up the list and contact the Ministers. David, tell the Captain that we will need a number of squads to place at their churches to protect those Ministers."

David asks, "Tell him?"

"Well, ask him."

Sam runs the list for Kenne and gives it to him a few minutes later.

"Lieutenant," he says. "There are one-hundred and thirty-two Seventh Day Adventist Churches in the county."

"You're kidding me," Kenne says in a startled voice.

"You'd better be right on this," Sam says shaking his head.

"Pass that information onto David so he can also ask the Captain for phone help."

A few minutes after David asked Captain Manning for reinforcements the Captain stormed into Kenne's office.

"What in hell is going on, now?" Manning asks.

Kenne hands The Fourth Commandment to Manning and says, "Read this."

Manning looks at the headline and says, "I know all about The Fourth Commandment."

"Just read it."

Manning sits down and reads the document.

"What's this got to do with the Domino killer?" Manning asks.

Kenne relates his story about spending the night at the office and how he came across this latest scenario. Manning shakes his head and heads for the door. He turns and says, "I used to think you were the best detective that ever graced our humble offices and sometimes (he raises his voice) I think you're as bizarre as a circus clown … I'll see what I can do."

****

Lamar and Bradley report back and give Kenne their findings.

"They all said the likenesses were similar to her looks but nobody picked out an exact likeness," Lamar informs Kenne. "However they all picked one as the closest."

Lamar hands Kenne the drawing.

"The person that gave us the best description on that sketch was Poe," Bradley states. "He said her nose was a bit larger, her chin wasn't as pointed and she had a fuller face."

"What about the booking photo?" Kenne asks.

"Nobody recognized it at being anything near what she looks like," Lamar answers.

"Lamar, have the artist make the changes Poe suggests and then run it by him," Kenne orders.

"Lieutenant. What's going on in the squad room? Who are all those people on phones?" Bradley asks.

"Never mind that," Kenne states. "We need to talk to Poe, again. You get him and I'll meet you in number one."

Poe moves slowly through the interrogation room door because his legs are shackled and he is handcuffed.

"Sit down," Kenne orders him.

After he sits down, Bradley takes a seat next to Kenne across the table from Poe. Bradley turns on a recorder.

"I need to know everything you know about the woman who calls herself Ana Trout," Kenne starts the interrogation.

"What's this?" Poe asks. "Why do you keep wanting information about Ana and why did I have to identify here picture?"

"Once again, I'll ask the questions," Kenne barks at him.

"It's in your best interest to answer the questions truthfully," Bradley apprises him. "We'll know if you're lying."

Kenne starts, "Did she ever discuss where she came from, her home town?"

"No," Poe says shaking his head.

"How about siblings? Did she ever mention any?"

"No."

"Tell me about her personality."

Poe hesitates for a moment before starting.

"Most of the time she was very friendly. A joy to be around with a sense of humor. Then, like I said before, she would have these mood swings. They were very ugly. She turned into a real bitch. That's how I kept getting into trouble with that domestic abuse stuff."

"How long did those mood swings last?" Bradley asks.

"Sometimes an hour or two. Sometimes a day."

"Any clue as to what brought them on?" Kenne asks. "Did you do or say something that set her off?"

"I really don't know," Poe answers with a puzzled look on his face.

"Was she taking any medication for those mood swings?" Kenne asks.

Poe shakes his head and says, "Not that I know of."

"What did you usually do when she went into one of these mood swings?" Bradley asks.

"Stay as far away from her as possible."

"Could the mood swings have been an act because she wanted to be alone?" Kenne asks.

"I don't know. I'm not a psychiatrist," Poe answers with contempt in his voice.

"What color are her eyes?" Bradley asks.

"Brown."

"Are you a murderer?" Kenne asks trying to prove his scenario of Poe being Domino. "Did you kill Victor De La Hoz and Ana Trout and then masquerade as a woman impersonating Trout?"

"I'm not a murderer and I'm surely not a damn transvestite. What the hell is going on here?"

"We'll let you know when it's time," Kenne says ending the interrogation.

****

When Captain Manning was in Kenne's office Kenne instructed him on the protection procedures he wanted followed to the letter. He wants two non-uniformed officers – three if it could be arranged – at every site. One officer is to stand at the front door of the church at all times while the other officer or officers shall patrol the area including the

259

rear of buildings. They are to watch for a figure, most likely a woman, dressed in black, wearing a hooded pullover sweat shirt. They are to arrive an hour before church time and report to the Minister.

During the church services one officer shall keep the Minister in site at all times. When the services are complete one officer shall remain at the Minister's side.

Captain Manning agreed to the procedures.

Sergeant Singleton enters Kenne's office while looking down at his list of churches.

He sits down and reports, "Most of the Ministers have been responsive to our phone calls and agree that non-uniformed officers is a good idea so as not to alarm the parishioners. A few of them regarded the phone call as a hoax. Every one of them said cancellation of services is not an option."

"Do you have a list of the naysayers?" Kenne asks.

Singleton hands Kenne his list and says, "They're marked with an 'X'."

Kenne looks over the list. There are six churches marked with an 'X' and the Minister's name appears next to the 'X'.

"I'll give them a call," Kenne says.

Just as they are finished, Captain Manning is standing in the doorway. As Singleton leaves, Manning sits down.

"Four-hundred men to catch one wacko woman," Manning says. "I had to recruit two-hundred and fifty L.A.P.D. officers to accomplice the protection for all those church Ministers. The county is going to receive a bill for the officer man hours used compliments of Mayor Kennelly."

"Mayor Kennelly is a jackass," Kenne comments. "And besides he doesn't like me."

"I'm beginning to wonder if I like you anymore."

"Come on Ray, you love me and you know it. You wouldn't know what to do without me."

Manning sits quietly and nods his head a few times.

Chapter 20

Officer Down

Kenne is finished pacing the floor waiting for the updated sketches from the art department. He calls them and gets somebody who knows nothing about it. Kenne describes the artist and he's told that he had to leave on a personal matter. His wife was giving birth to their first child. Kenne informs the young lady that he's talking too that he's on the way there.

The art department is on the third floor in the east wing of the building. The young lady he talked to on the phone greets him at the door. She explains that another artist will be working on the project, immediately.

"Not without my help," Kenne informs her.

"Helene Porter will be doing the work. Follow me."

Kenne follows the young lady into a small office off to the right. Porter is sitting at a drawing table. Kenne walks over and stands behind her and describes the changes he wants to the sketch. As Porter makes the changes, Kenne gives her some minor instructions on other changes. Once he's satisfied with the facial structure of the sketch he asks Porter to give her three different hairstyles which he describes. Satisfied with the outcome of the sketches Kenne heads for the lockup to show the sketches to Poe. Poe identifies all three sketches as look a likes but the one with her hair down to her shoulders is the hairdo she wore when he knew her. The other two sketches show short hair and long hair.

When Kenne arrives back at the squad room, Dave is on the phone. He gives Kenne the high sign to come over. Dave hangs up the phone and looks at Kenne.

"We've got an officer down," Dave says.

"Where?"

"At a church in Culver City."

"Come on," Kenne orders as he heads for the door.

Dave follows him.

****

Church services were in session when Kenne and Dave arrived at the church on Washington Boulevard in Culver City. Mac and Ramirez are already there as they were out cruising when the call came in on the radio. There are three L.A.P.D. police cars on the scene and a fire department ambulance.

Kenne asks Mac, "How's the officer?"

"He's in the ambulance waiting to be transported to Los Angeles County Hospital.

It looks like he's going to be okay. I held them up until you got here."

"Good thinking," Kenne commends her as they walk toward the ambulance.

Mac continues, "His name is Barney Clifford. He was attacked near the back door of the church. He was hit in the head from behind with a rock. Alphonso found the rock and put it in the car. It's pretty much covered with Clifford's blood.

Kenne enters the ambulance and sits down on a bench next to Clifford who is being attended by a paramedic. He is awake and talking to the paramedic.

"Can I talk to him?" Kenne asks the paramedic.

"Yeah. But make it fast. They're waiting for him at the hospital."

"Officer Clifford, I'm Lieutenant Quint-cannon with the county sheriff's department. I've got a few questions for you."

"I know who you are," Clifford says turning his head and looking at Kenne.

"Are you up to it?"

"Go ahead. I'm okay. I know we need to do this."

"What can you tell me about your attacker?" Kenne asks.

"It was a woman. She was small. About a hundred and twenty pounds. She attacked me from behind and just before she hit me hard with a blunt instrument I saw her out of the corner of my eye and defended myself the best I could. That's probably why I got hit in the side of the head with a glancing blow off my shoulder."

Clifford pauses for a moment from an episode of dizziness.

He continues, "She was wearing a black-hooded sweat shirt. As I was falling to the ground I ripped the hood off her head. After I hit the ground I kicked her pretty hard in her shin on the left leg. She was limping when she ran away. After that I guess I passed out. One of my partners was attending to me when I woke up. I was kind of dizzy and out of it until the paramedics got here."

"He's suffering from a probable concussion," the paramedic says.

Kenne pulls the sketches out of his jacket pocket and shows them to Clifford.

"Do you recognize any of these women as your attacker?" Kenne asks.

"No. Not at all."

Kenne shows him Ana Trout's booking photo and asks, "How about her?"

"Yeah. That might be her. I know when I pulled the hood off her head I did notice she had blonde hair and it was all messed up and she didn't have any makeup on."

"Could the blonde hair been a wig?" Kenne continues with the questions.

"Yeah. That's possible. When I pulled the hood off it looked like her hair was coming with it."

Kenne flashes Ana Trout's yellow sheet mug shot in front of him again, and says, "Be sure. Is this her?"

Clifford nods his head, "I really didn't get a good look at her face. Everything got kind of fuzzy after I was hit."

Kenne pats Clifford on his leg and says, "Thanks. You did good."

Ramirez is waiting for Kenne when he exits the ambulance. He waves a computer disc in Kenne's face.

"Do you know what this is?" Ramirez asks.

"A video of Led Zeppelin's last concert?" Kenne answers in a sarcastic tone knowing that Ramirez is a big fan.

"Very funny," Ramirez says. "The church has a security camera mounted on the rear of the building. This disc is from that security camera. Do you care to look at it?"

Kenne grabs the disc and walks to his squad car. He slides the disc into his video recorder in the dashboard. He fast forwards to the spot of the attack and Kenne and Ramirez watch the video. The video shows a distant and distorted image of the attacker's face.

Kenne releases the video from the recorder and hands it to Ramirez.

"Have forensics blow her face up so we can identify her. I don't care if it takes them all night. I want a clear image on my desk in the morning."

Ramirez sits and looks at Kenne.

"Go!" Kenne shouts.

Dave is driving Kenne's squad car on the way back to the office while Kenne is staring at the different sketches.

"There could be a hundred or more women who look like this," Kenne says. "Do any of these images look familiar to you?"

Kenne holds them up one at a time. Dave shifts his eyes back and forth between the road and the sketches.

"I've got a cousin on my mother's side that looks a bit like them, but she lives in Texas, now," Dave answers.

Kenne holds the one with short hair up and says, "This one does but the hair style is different and she has blue eyes, not brown."

He shrugs his shoulders and continues, "I'm probably just imagining things."

"Why don't you have that artist do some sketches with different short-hair hair styles and blue eyes when we get back to head-quarters," Dave suggests.

Kenne takes Dave's advice and his first mission when he returns to headquarters is to pay another visit to Helene Porter in the art department. With Kenne's help she sketches other images changing the hair style and giving her blue eyes. Kenne looks at the finished sketches and thanks Porter.

He then rushes to see the communication center and asks Nikki Cox to distribute all of the sketches along with Trout's yellow sheet mug shot to the print media and television stations.

Chapter Twenty-One

Dysfunctional Ancestry

As Kenne is walking through the squad room toward his office Detective McDonald informs him there is an FBI agent waiting for him. Kenne nods his head toward Mac as if to say thank you. The agent is Parker Cunningham. They greet each other with a strong handshake and Kenne offers him a seat.

"What's up?" Kenne asks. "What are you doing here?"

"I've got an interesting tale to tell you."

"I'm all ears," Kenne quips.

Cunningham has been holding a rolled up sheet of paper in his left hand. He opens it so he can refer to it.

"I had my Atlanta office do some extensive research. To start, your Ana Trout didn't travel to Atlanta two years ago to take care of a sick mother. She went there to bury her grandmother."

Using the sheet of paper as a reference he continues, "They found a death certificate for a Caroline Bainbridge dated August twenty-sixth, two years ago. Further investigation of Caroline's past turned up a birth certificate of a Lea Bainbridge that listed Caroline as the mother but no identification of the father.

"Digging deeper they found that Albert Hill was probably Lea's father. Lea got married in 1980 to a Peter Featherstone of Seminole Indian heritage. This guy had a felony record dating back to when he was twelve years old. Anyhow, they had one child, a girl, born in 1982, named Priscilla. Back to her in a moment.

"Lea Featherstone died in a facility for the insane in 1986. Peter Featherstone moved back to the Seminole reservation shortly after Lea's death. He got involved with some more felonious activity and was killed in 1989 fleeing the scene of a bank robbery."

"Are you leading up to Priscilla Firestone taking the name Ana Trout as an alias?" Kenne says.

"Wait a minute. I've got a lot more," Cunningham says evading Kenne's question. "Getting back to Priscilla. She was married at age eighteen to a Carlos Navarro, a man in his thirties. About a year later he disappeared and was believed to be dead. A body was never found. Six months later Priscilla married a man named Anthony Giavatella. He too disappeared about a year later under mysterious circumstances. Once again, a body was never found.

"The Atlanta police suspected Priscilla of the murder of both husbands but had no concrete proof. Knowing that the police were watching her, she decided to disappear, also. However, she took a different route than normal. She paid a visit to an old high school friend by the name of Ana Trout."

"You've got my undivided attention," Kenne interrupts.

"I figured so," Cunningham quips. "Continuing. The real Ana Trout disappeared never to be found. Then years later Ana Trout, or should I say Priscilla Featherstone shows up in California impersonating Ana Trout. Apparently, Priscilla absconded with Ana Trout's identification. We ran a check with the Social Security Administration and lo and behold it turns out the duplicate number you have for Ana Trout and Jason Poe is the real Ana Trout's number."

"Did you happen to get a history of her job locations?" Kenne asks.

"I did better than that. I got a printout from the IRS of all of her past W-2's and 1099's from the time the real Ana Trout disappeared. The real weird thing is she was actually filing an income tax every year up until the time she probably duplicated the number and gave it to Poe."

"Do you have a copy for me?"

"I'll email you one."

Kenne grabs the latest sketch of Ana Trout and shows it to Cunningham.

"Do you recognize her?" Kenne asks.

"No," Cunningham answers shaking his head.

"Unfortunately, I do," Kenne says in a soft tone. "Can you believe a good looking girl like this comes from a dysfunctional family?"

"If that's Priscilla Featherstone, I believe she not only continued but also added another page to her family's dysfunction," Cunningham states. "If Ana Trout is Priscilla Featherstone then I've got some information for you my friend."

"What's that?" Kenne asks.

"She's committed murder across state lines. That makes this a Federal offense and I have jurisdiction."

"Let me get this straight. You want to take over the case?"

"Not exactly."

"What does that mean?" Kenne asks with a puzzled look on his face.

"This has been your case from the beginning and I don't want to interfere with that. So, what it means is that I'm going to work with you in apprehending Ana Trout or should I call her Priscilla Featherstone."

Kenne nods his head in agreement and says, "You know something. I believe we're going to become good friends."

Both men smile at each other.

Kenne asks, "Can I see that sheet of paper?"

Cunningham hands Kenne his reference paper. Kenne places it on the desk and spends some time looking at it. After a few minutes he picks up a pen and starts circling words on the paper. He has circled the name Lea, the Gia in the name Giavatella and the Na in the name Navarro. He then writes the circled letters on the bottom of the paper. They spell Giana Lea. He strikes out the a in Lea and replaces it with an e. It now reads Giana Lee. Kenne hands the paper back to Cunningham.

"That's Ana Trout's current name," he tells Cunningham.

"How do you know that?"

"Remember when I said I recognize the face on the sketch?"

"I remember."

"I've been in denial and also sleeping with her for the last few weeks."

"What?" Cunningham says, flabbergasted.

"I met her … no … she picked me up at the Westwood Sports Lounge one night. She came on to me like a linebacker sacking a quarterback. I had a hard day and needed a diversion and she was it."

"Where is she now?" Cunningham asks.

"I don't know. I don't think she'd go back to her apartment. She's got to know we're on to her. You know, I asked her to go to Palm Springs for the weekend and she declined. She said she had another commitment. Looks like her commitment was to kill a church minister."

"Wait a second," Cunningham says. "Something you just said. She's got to know we're on to her. How does she know that?"

"I don't know. Maybe she's realized we're smarter than she is."

"Do you talk in your sleep?" Cunningham asks.

"Not that I know of. How does one know if they talk in their sleep when they're sleeping at the time?" Kenne answers with a question of his own.

Cunningham holds up his index finger on his right hand and looks around Kenne's office.

"What are you looking for?' Kenne asks.

"A good place to put a wire. Has Giana ever been in your office?"

"No."

Cunningham thinks for a moment and then says, "Tuesday, in Glendale, you were wearing that sports jacket. When's the last time you changed jackets?"

"I don't know. A couple weeks ago. It's my favorite."

"Take it off," Cunningham says.

Kenne stands up and takes his jacket off. Cunningham grabs it and pulls the lapel back. There is a small microphone attached with a safety pin. Cunningham removes the microphone and sets it on the desk.

"I believe that's how she knows you're on to her. She came on to you because she knew you were handling the Domino case and she wanted to know your every step. She's one smart chick."

"I'll be damned," Kenne comments sitting back down in his chair. "But, why the change in looks? Why not just wear a mask?"

"That's a question that we need to find an answer for."

Chapter Twenty-Two

All-Points

Kenne Narration: "My pride was scorched knowing that Giana had duped me so easily. But I'll recover. I started my recovery process by instructing the communications department to issue an all-points bulletin on Giana. I advised them to use both the latest sketch of Giana and her yellow sheet mug shot for identification purposes. Along with that I gave them the description of her vehicle. A 2008 brown Ford Focus. I didn't have the license number but I had Sam checking with DMV for a possible auto registration. I also had communications highlight the fact that she may be hobbled with a leg injury. That was the easy part. After that I requested a dragnet procedure put into effect from Captain Manning. Manning told me that he would take the request to Sheriff Unger because his approval was needed.

"Even though it was Saturday night, I was able to obtain a search warrant and I asked Mac, Bradley and Lamar to join me in a search of Giana's apartment. My request was met with a number of groans but they all relented when I promised to furnish donuts in the morning. Agent Cunningham volunteered himself and three of his agents to join us. I wonder if he promised them donuts, too."

Just as Kenne expected, Giana was not home. Detective Bradley kicked in the door. Kenne was the first one to enter. He has his department issue Glock G43 drawn and pointing. He looks around very carefully and then makes his way to the bedroom to make sure Giana isn't there. Bradley is following close behind.

"Nobody's here," Bradley turns and informs everyone.

Kenne and Agent Cunningham stand in the living quarters and watch as the three detectives and three FBI agents search the apartment. After a few minutes Mac calls Kenne into the bedroom. Cunningham follows him. The first thing Kenne notices is the mattress and bedspring have been tossed off the bed. Before Kenne can walk over there Lamar intercepts him and shows him two black-hooded sweat shirts and an empty box.

"Lieutenant, these were in this box on the closet shelf," Lamar states.

"Hold them as evidence," Kenne instructs him.

Lying out in the open now that the mattress and bedspring have been removed are three deadly weapons. A garden shears, sickle and small ax along with an unopened bottle of rat poison.

"Jesus," Kenne comments. "She was going to use these in future attacks.

"What's the rat poison for?" Mac asks.

"Probably for herself if she got cornered," Kenne answers.

"That stuff tastes terrible," Bradley opines.

"How do you know that?" Lamar asks.

"Rats hate the taste. They drop dead from it," Bradley says with a giggle.

Cunningham looks at Kenne with a puzzled look on his face.

"I have to put up with this every day," Kenne says to Cunningham. "It's part of the job."

Cunningham shakes his head and says, "You've got my sympathy."

Lying next to the weapons are a 'Line of Play' dominoes sitting on a plywood board. They are identical to the 'Line of Play' dominoes on the table in the squad room. In a case nearby is the remainder of the set. The set is white with black pips which is opposite of the dominoes left at the scene of the crimes. There is a white sealed envelope sitting on the board. It is addressed – To: Lieutenant Quintcannon. Kenne opens it and pulls a hand written note and reads it. He hands the note to Mac.

"Read it out loud," Kenne instructs her.

"I've got the rest of the other set. Piece by piece I will deliver them to you," she reads.

Cunningham says, "It looks like she's still open for business."

Kenne walks over to the closet and starts rifling through the hanging clothes. He determines there are a lot of clothes that don't fit Giana's image. He decides they probably belong to her sister. Then he stops. Cunningham said Giana … Priscilla was an only child. He shakes his head while thinking it doesn't make sense.

One of Cunningham's agents enters the bedroom and announces, "We've found a pretty sophisticated computer system in the roll top desk in the living room. Wasserman is disassembling it for removable."

"Grab any software lying around, also," Cunningham instructs him.

Kenne turns his attention to the weapons and dominoes and instructs his squad to collect them as evidence.

Mac stoops over to collect the dominoes – one at a time – and realizes they are glued to the plywood.

"Lieutenant," she says. "The domino tiles are glued down."

"Then take the whole board," Kenne instructs.

Another of Cunningham's agents enters the bedroom and says, "Parker, you need to come see this."

Cunningham and Kenne follow the agent into the kitchen. The cabinet doors beneath the sink are open and the agent points to a garbage container. Cunningham looks inside and then motions Kenne over to look. Inside the container is a pair of medical gloves. Cunningham instructs his agent to recover them and hold them as evidence.

Another agent is trying to pull finger prints from around the room.

"Anything yet?" Cunningham asks.

"I've got some partials but I've got a long way to go," the agent answers.

"Be sure to check the refrigerator," Cunningham suggests.

Kenne and Cunningham are riding together in Kenne's squad car on the way back to headquarters.

"Some of those clothes in the closet just don't fit Giana's image," Kenne says.

"Where are you going with that?" Cunningham asks.

"Giana told me she had a sister that would stay with her from time to time. But you said Ana didn't have any siblings."

"When did she tell you this?"

"Just after I called her to cash in a rain check …"

"A rain check?" Cunningham asks with a funny look on his face.

"It's not important. Anyhow, the first time I called the voice on the other end sounded a lot like Giana but she said I got a wrong number. Later on I told Giana about the wrong number and she said it was her sister. She told me she comes and goes without warning. That she was a flight attendant and only came around when she was in town or something like that."

"There is no sister," Cunningham says. "Remember, Priscilla was an only child."

"That's why those clothes bother me."

"Did she happen to mention the airline this supposed sister worked for?"

"Delta."

"Do you have a name for this sister?"

"I believe she said Eliana, Eliana Lee," Kenne answers.

Cunningham grabs his cell phone out of his jacket pocket and calls his office. He instructs the voice on the other end to check out the information Kenne gave him on Eliana. Meanwhile, Kenne uses his cell phone to call Dr. Goldstein to ask him to come to his office. Goldstein says that he'll be there in the morning.

****

Even though it's Sunday, Kenne's entire squad showed up for the donuts. Kenne and Agent Cunningham joined them before retiring to Kenne's office. A short time later Dr. Goldstein arrives and grabs a donut and cup of coffee before heading to Kenne's office.

It takes Kenne and Cunningham ten minutes to update Goldstein on the Domino case. Goldstein sits silent for a few minutes as he finishes eating his donut and sipping at the hot coffee. He keeps glancing back and forth at Kenne and Cunningham while thinking. The two men stare impatiently at Goldstein waiting for his opinion.

Goldstein breaks the silence, "It's possible … I'm only saying it's possible we are dealing with a woman with multiple personalities. The medical term is dissociative identity disorder or D-I-D."

Kenne and Cunningham look at each other with stunned looks on their faces.

"You mean like that three faces of Eve thing?" Kenne asks.

Goldstein nods his head and says, "More like a Dr. Jekyll and Mr. Hyde thing. Or should I say Miss Hyde."

"How many personalities are we dealing with, here?" Cunningham asks.

Goldstein shrugs his shoulders, "Who knows? But, more than likely only two."

"If this is true, which personality is the serial killer?" Kenne asks.

Goldstein shakes his head and mutters, "I wouldn't have a clue until I have a chance to talk to her. Then again, with her I.Q. we may never know unless she volunteers the information."

"Unfortunately, talking to her isn't possible right now," Kenne says. "What if you talked to Poe? Do you think he could help?"

"I don't think so."

"Doctor, can you tell us more about this multiple personality thing?" Cunningham asks.

Goldstein laughs.

"It's not that simple. I'm not an expert on the subject but I'll try," Goldstein answers. "D-I-D is one of the most controversial psychiatric disorders known and there is no diagnostic criteria or treatment. It has no relationship to schizophrenia. A study estimated there is between one and three percent of the population that suffer from D-I-D."

Wrrrew Kenne whistles, "That's quite a large number."

Goldstein continues, "That's not all. If I remember correctly, D-I-D is three to nine times more prevalent in females."

"What causes it?" Cunningham asks.

"It could be anything but most likely it's the result of a traumatic childhood, but not necessarily. The symptoms usually surface at a young age but can also start as a young adult. However, there can be other more complicated causes.

"If you really want to know the history, diagnosis and pathophysiology of D-I-D, you can probably find it under the subject dissociative identity disorder on the internet."

"Giana ... or should I say Priscilla ... has used four different identities," Kenne states. "Does this mean she has four different personalities?"

"Like I said, probably not. If she was a suspect in her two husband's murders it was probably just the start. She used the Ana Trout identity to create the disappearance of Priscilla. Then she changed her name to Giana Lee when she perpetrated the Domino scenario. The invention of a sister is a method of hiding the split personality. It could be she used other aliases and committed other murders while assuming the other identities along the way."

Kenne excuses himself and asks Sam to run the D-I-D information on the internet with three copies. Just as Kenne returns to his office, Cunningham's cell phone rings. He answers and talks for a few minutes.

After the conclusion of the call he informs Kenne, "Delta Airlines have no record of an Eliana Lee, Giana Lee, Ana Trout or Priscilla Featherstone ever working for them in any capacity."

"Marv, tell me if this is logical thinking," Kenne says. "The Giana personality is protective of the Eliana personality. It was Giana's idea to dupe me so that Eliana knew our every move."

"So, you think Eliana is the serial killer," Goldstein comments. "Another logical idea is that the Eliana personality coaxed Giana into duping you. That would mean Eliana is the controlling personality. Then on the other hand Giana could be the dominant personality and the serial killer and Eliana is the one with the high I.Q. and coaxing her to commit murder."

Kenne looks at Goldstein in awe.

Cunningham interrupts, "Then again, there could be a hundred other scenarios. Isn't that right, Doctor?"

Goldstein nods his head and says, "Precisely."

Sam enters the office and hands each of the men a copy of his D-I-D internet printout.

"There's fourteen pages, there," he informs them and leaves the room.

All three thumb through the information and Goldstein finally says, "Read through this information and it will give you an educated idea of what you're dealing with. One sick lady. You also need a session or two with an expert on the subject."

"Do you know one?" Cunningham asks.

"Doctor Patricia Winslow with the Clinic for Dissociative Identity Disorders located right here in Los Angeles."

Chapter Twenty-Three

The Battle of Wits Begins

Kenne Narration: "When I woke up on Monday morning I realized my midsection was starting to suffer from a lack of exercise so I called Harley and asked him to meet me at Venice Beach for a session of competitive basketball. He agreed in a heartbeat."

Both men are exhausted after a two-hour workout and collapse on a nearby bench. They are both breathing heavy and trying to inhale oxygen from the ninety-five degree heat.

"I feel like I'm having a heart attack," Kenne says gasping for air.

"You too," Harley says gasping for air, also.

They both sit for a while until they can breathe normal.

"That was some workout," Kenne says.

"Yeah, but we both needed it."

A gust of super-heated air blows off the ocean picking up loose sand from the beach and hitting both men square in the face. They wipe the sand off their sweat drenched faces and laugh.

"A gust of sand filled hot air to top off the day," Harley says.

"I've had worse," Kenne comments.

"Speaking of worse. How's your case shaping up?"

"Have you got about twenty minutes?"

"I've got the rest of the day," Harley answers.

It took Kenne seventeen minutes to update Harley on the Domino case. After he was finished both men sat quiet for a few minutes until Harley broke the silence.

"That's quite a story. I've got a similar one for you."

"Really."

"It was about three-years ago. One of my former college classmates was coaching women's volleyball at a local community college. He called me and explained he was having trouble with one of his top players and he asked me to attend their next game. The girl in question was the captain and star of the team.

"Nothing unusual happened and she was at her best until the final minute. It was as if the devil was inside her. She became a raving maniac. She started cussing at her teammates if they made a mistake or at the referees for no reason. But the worst of it was the foul language trash talk toward the opponents.

"Of course, the referees had to eject her from the game. Afterwards, the coach asked me to join him in the locker room. All the team members were sitting on benches near their lockers except for our subject. She was dressed and standing by the exit door. The coach asked her to step over by us and she gave him the finger and walked out. The coach asked me what I thought and I couldn't give him an answer.

"I was dumfounded by her actions. Then I remembered a class I took in my senior year about dissociative identity disorder and thought that might be the girl's problem. I remember calling a Doctor Winslow in on the matter and she asked to examine the girl. The coach went to her mother and explained what was going on and got permission for Doctor Winslow to examine her.

"Anyhow, Winslow determined the girl had D-I-D and hospitalized her. Somewhere around eighteen months later the girl was cured. What therapy Doctor Winslow did to cure her was never revealed. Doctor, patient confidentiality."

"I've got an appointment with Winslow first thing tomorrow morning," Kenne states.

"If anybody can figure out what's going on in Domino's head, Winslow can. She's the best."

"Did Winslow ever relate the causes of the girl's bout with D-I-D?" Kenne asks.

"Actually, no. But I got the probable cause from the mother. Winslow determined the girl had a normal childhood until the age of thirteen. It was then that one of her mother's boyfriends raped her over and over and over. It traumatized her and her personality changed for the worse. The girl's brain then created the sweet personality to help her cope with the rapes. However, the girl's original personality would come out from time to time and set her off, uncontrollably. That's what was causing her irrational actions.

"The mother also told me that her daughter would have to be on medicine the rest of her life."

"Sounds like Winslow knows her business," Kenne remarks.

"If Winslow lets you sit in on some sessions, pay strict attention. You'll learn a lot. That is if you catch Domino alive. And another thing. Some good advice. You need to start checking out your lady friends before you sleep with them."

Kenne Narration: "My good friend, Harley. Always with the advice. Maybe, this time I should listen to him."

* * * * * * * * * *

On his way home, Kenne stopped at the office mainly to see if Captain Manning was able to convince Sheriff Unger that a dragnet needed to be set in place. Manning had left for the day but Sam was still there and he gave Kenne the bad news that a dragnet was out of the question. The cost was too prohibitive and there aren't enough funds in the budget for so costly an agenda.

But Sam did give him some good news. Besides Giana's picture being in the evening newspapers and television breaking news segments, the internet was loaded with all of her images. Also Agent Cunningham called and left two messages. One, that the FBI has listed Giana Lee as public enemy number one in the Los Angeles section. The second message was the partial print they found was of Giana's middle finger on the right hand. It had enough points to match Ana Trout's booking finger print.

Kenne's meeting with Dr. Winslow on Monday morning was short but informative about D-I-D afflicted people. She also explained to Kenne that she couldn't get involved in the case until Giana was caught and she could administer a therapy program for her. Kenne explained to Dr. Winslow that he wouldn't be arresting her so she could go through therapy. He'd be arresting her so she could keep an appointment with the gas chamber.

On his arrival at his office later that morning the message light is flashing on his office telephone. He pushes the message button and listens.

"Good morning, Lieutenant. Sorry I wasn't able to leave you a souvenir the other day. But I promise to make up for it, soon. After all, we must finish the game."

****

Giana is looking in a mirror and combing her hair in a motel room in Arcadia. The motel room number is 4. She has cut her hair very short and dyed it red and she is not wearing any makeup. A reflection in the mirror shows a naked man in the bed behind her. There is a bathroom towel over his face and he is lying in a pool of blood. A handle of a large paring knife is sticking up on the left side of his chest.

Giana picks up a domino lying on the credenza underneath the mirror and walks over to the body and places it in the right hand and pats the corpse on the head.

She turns and looks in the mirror one more time and says to herself out loud, "Eliana was here. I can't protect her anymore. She's driving me crazy."

296

With that Giana's whole body shakes for about fifteen seconds and her personality disappears. She is now Eliana, forever.

It's six-thirty in the evening when Eliana leaves the motel room with a suitcase and drives away in a blue Dodge Ram 1500 pickup truck with New Mexico plates. She drives around on city streets for awhile and grabs some dinner at the drive through of a fast food restaurant. Then she drives to a nearby park and eats her dinner. When she's finished she heads for Santa Monica as the sun is setting.

****

Kenne is still in his office at headquarters when the phone rings in the squad room. He rushes to his doorway and stands there as Lamar answers the phone. Lamar listens and nods his head and thanks the caller before hanging up.

He looks at Kenne and informs him, "They found her car."

Kenne and Lamar leave the squad room in a rush and head for a shopping center on Las Tunas Drive in Temple City where Giana's car was abandoned.

The shopping center in Temple City has six businesses with a large grocery chain as its anchor. Kenne confirms that the car is Giana's. He and Lamar conduct an exhaustive search of the vehicle looking for anything that would indicate where Giana has gone from there. They come up with nothing so Kenne directs the two Temple City police officers who found the car to have it towed to the county impound yard.

"Let's check out the stores. Maybe someone saw her," Kenne says to Lamar.

Two of the six stores are closed. After looking at the type of businesses in the center, Kenne decides to start with the grocery store. They ask for the manager upon entering the store and stopping at the customer service counter.

The night manager greets them and when Kenne flashes his badge and tells him why they're here he agrees to let them talk to his employees. Kenne and Lamar start with the checkout cashiers. They show each one Giana's sketch and booking photo. One of the clerks responds that she thinks she checked her out as she points to Giana's sketch.

"Do you remember what she bought?" Kenne asks.

"Just a few items."

"Please try and remember the items. Was it all food or maybe some personal items?"

"Yeah. I remember one personal item. A box of hair color. At the time I thought why would she want to change her hair color. Her hair looked fine just the way it was."

"Do you remember the color?" Kenne continues with the questions.

"Red," the clerk responds in a positive voice.

"How did she pay you?"

"Cash."

"Did you notice anything about her appearance? The clothes she was wearing and like that?"

"Not really. But she was talking to the man in line behind her. I remember she introduced herself and he continued the conversation. After I was finished checking her out, she waited for the man and they left the store together."

"Do you remember what items he bought?"

"Just some microwave fast foods and a six-pack of beer."

"How did he pay you?"

"Cash. He had a big wad that he pulled out of his pocket. The smallest bill I noticed was a twenty."

"How was he dressed?"

"He had a cowboy hat on. A blue shirt and blue jeans. I think he was wearing cowboy boots."

"How tall was he?"

"He was tall. Six-four, maybe six-five and he was well built."

"How old do you think he was?"

"I don't know. Maybe in his forties."

Kenne looks out the windows of the store front and says, "One more question. Did you happen to see what kind of vehicle they drove away in?"

"I was kind of busy and never thought to look."

"Thank you for your time," Kenne says.

Kenne walks away without saying a word and Lamar follows him.

Kenne and Lamar sit in the squad car and talk.

"She picked up that guy for three reasons," Kenne declares.

"What three reasons?" Lamar asks.

"Money, more money and his vehicle," Kenne answers as he nods his head toward the right.

"You think she intends on killing the dude?" Lamar asks.

"I think she already did. It's just a matter of finding the body."

"How about a nearby motel," Lamar remarks.

"How about that," Kenne responds.

Kenne leaves the car in a rush and goes into a real estate office that is still open. He comes out a few minutes later with a number of telephone book pages in his hand.

Kenne hands Lamar half of them and instructs him, "Look for small motels. No large chains."

After checking out four motels with no success, they pull into an eight room motel parking lot in Arcadia. Kenne looks around and notices the rooms are numbered one to eight.

"Number four. Let's go talk to the manager," Kenne says.

The manager is a short Japanese man. He informs Kenne that a woman that looks like Giana's sketch rented number four yesterday.

"For how long?" Kenne asks.

"Just two days."

"Was she alone?"

"Yes."

"Tell me. Why did you place her in number four?"

"She requested it. In fact, she said four was her lucky number and if she couldn't get that room she wasn't interested in staying here."

"How did she pay you?"

"Cash. I don't usually deal in cash but she paid me a hundred dollar security deposit. It was her idea so I would accept the cash."

"The room looks dark," Kenne says. "Do you think she's there now?"

"I don't know."

"Grab your pass key and come with us," Kenne instructs the manager.

After they knock and there is no answer the manager unlocks the door to room 4 and steps aside. Kenne and Lamar enter with guns drawn. The first thing they notice is the dead man on the bed.

"Don't let him in here," Kenne instructs Lamar.

Lamar closes the door behind him.

Kenne walks over to the right side of the bed and immediately notices the domino in the victim's right hand. He removes the domino and places it in jacket pocket. As he does so he notices the numbers on the dominoes sides. They are four and two.

"Search the entire unit," Kenne instructs Lamar. "We're looking for I.D., money and maybe a cell phone."

While Lamar follows his instructions, Kenne calls Coroner Fong and his forensics department to report the murder and ask for their assistance.

Meanwhile, Lamar opens all the drawers in the credenza and bedside tables, and then looks in the closet and the bathroom. When finished he reports to Kenne.

"Nothing. The place is clean. His clothes aren't here, either"

"What about under the bed?" Kenne asks.

Lamar gets down on his knees and looks under the bed.

"Just dust," he comments.

Kenne leaves the room and approaches the manager who is waiting outside.

"What's going on in there?" the manager asks.

"At the moment, nothing," Kenne evasively answers not wanting to upset the manager. "The woman in 4 had a visitor earlier in the evening. Did you happen to notice what kind of vehicle he was driving?"

"No. I was in the back room watching television."

"We'll be here for awhile and I've got some people coming so why don't you go back to your television programs."

Coroner Fong, who only lives ten minutes away is first to arrive. He knocks on the door of unit 4 once and then enters. He looks at the body on the bed and then at Kenne.

"You keeping him company," Fong jokes.

"Yeah, but only until you got here," Kenne jokes back.

"When are you going to find this maniac? She's ruining my love life," Fong continues with the jokes.

Kenne laughs and quips back, "Since when have you had a love life?"

Fong looks at Kenne with wrath in his eyes and says, "That's the trouble with you damn detectives. You know everything."

Kenne, Fong and Lamar all laugh.

Fong walks over to the body and shakes his head.

"That's a paring knife. What in hell was she thinking, that's he's a rump roast?" Fong continues with his jokes.

Kenne and Lamar look at each other and both shrug their shoulders.

After a few minutes of examining the body Fong reports the results, "Stabbed four times in the heart. First thrust probably killed him. I'll have my report on your desk in the morning."

Just as Fong is finished the forensic team arrives. Kenne asks them to have a report on his desk in the morning, as well.

Kenne also tells them, "It's imperative we get his prints. We really need to know who he is. Domino has his vehicle and we need to identify it."

****

Kenne and Lamar start making their way back to headquarters when Kenne's cellphone rings. It's Agent Cunningham. He informs Kenne about another victim at the hands of Domino. The attack occurred on Sixth Street in Santa Monica. Kenne tells

Cunningham he's on his way and also informs him about his victim in Arcadia.

After Kenne hangs up he calls Fong's cellphone and informs him of the Santa Monica incident and asks for his assistance. Fong isn't happy about a long drive to Santa Monica but he relents and tells Kenne he'll meet him there as soon as he's finished with the Arcadia mess.

There is a yellow-tape-crime scene ribbon wound around trees in a sixty-foot circumference where the body lies when Kenne arrives in Santa Monica. He immediately spots Cunningham talking to a uniformed Santa Monica policeman and walks over to him. Cunningham greets him and introduces the policeman. He is Santa Monica Police Captain Hiram Webster. Kenne and Webster shake hands.

"What are you doing here?" Kenne asks Cunningham."

Cunningham points to an old lady sitting in his car.

"That lady witnessed the attack and called 9-1-1 on her cell. The 9-1-1 operator called the Santa Monica police and my good friend Hiram called me thinking that I might be interested. Oh, yeah. She took a picture of Domino with her cell."

"You're kidding."

"No."

Kenne looks over at the victim. The body is covered with a blanket.

"We are able to identify the victim," Cunningham tells Kenne. "It seems Domino didn't have time to rifle through his pants and left without taking his wallet and money with her. And she did leave this."

Cunningham hands Kenne a domino. He looks at it for a moment as if memorizing the numbers on each side. They are two and one.

"Can I talk to our star witness?" Kenne asks Webster.

"Her name is Edith Cummings."

Kenne walks over to Cunningham's car and introduces himself to Edith.

She smiles at him and asks, "Are you with the FBI, too?"

"No. I'm with the County Sheriff's Department. Do you mind if I ask you a few questions?"

"Go right ahead," she says.

"What was the assailant wearing?"

"One of those hooded things."

"A hooded sweat shirt?"

"That could have been it."

"Was it black?"

"Yes, it was."

"After the attack, what did the assailant do?"

"He bent over and placed something in the young man's hand, then ran away that way."

She points to the east.

"When did you take the picture?"

"Just before he ran away, he looked at me and waved."

"Did you happen to see a vehicle that the assailant might have gotten into?"

"No. He just disappeared behind the buildings."

"The assailant isn't a he. It's a woman," Kenne informs Edith.

"Oh, my," she exclaims.

"Can I borrow your cellphone for a minute?"

"Sure," she agrees and hands Kenne the cellphone.

Kenne pulls his cellphone out of his pocket and transfers the picture from Edith's phone to his. He hands her cellphone back to her and places a kiss on her forehead.

"Thank you," Kenne says. "You've been a big help. My assistant is going to get your name, address and phone number if that's okay with you?"

She nods her head as Kenne signals for Ramirez.

Fong arrives and walks straight to the blanket covered body. Kenne follows him. Fong pulls the blanket off of the victim. He is a young man in his twenties and dressed in a jogging outfit. Kenne leaves Fong alone to do his job.

When he is finished Fong walks over to Kenne and gives his report.

"He was stabbed six times in the stomach and upper chest. Looks like the instrument was a smaller version of the Arcadia instrument. Probably both knives come from the same set."

"Any knife in the area?" Kenne asks.

"Not unless one of the policemen picked it up."

"That's highly unlikely, but I'll check."

Kenne asks around about the knife. Apparently, Domino took it with her.

****

The next morning Kenne is sitting at his desk wondering where Domino will strike again. He is stressed out with very little sleep the last two nights and is in a daze thinking Domino changed the application of the blank four side domino when she wasn't able to leave it with a victim. Instead, she gave that domino a new meaning by stabbing victim number eighteen four times in room four of some godforsaken motel. Then leaving the four two sides domino and killing victim nineteen by stabbing him six times on Sixth Street in Santa Monica. Then she left a two one sides domino with victim nineteen and Kenne is racking his brain trying to find what that domino represents.

Kenne's cellphone is sitting on his desk and its ringing breaks his daze. He answers it on the second ring. It's Steve Lockwood from the New Mexico Highway Patrol headquarters in Santa Fe. Lockwood and Kenne befriended each other when they were at the Los Angeles Police Academy.

"Kenne, it's Steve from New Mexico," the familiar voice informs him.

"Hey, buddy," Kenne responds. "You only call me when you need something. What's up?"

"I've got a lady here in my office whose husband went to L.A. a few days ago about buying some race horse foals and she hasn't heard from him," Steve gives Kenne the tale why he is calling.

"Ask her if he was going to Santa Anita?" Kenne asks.

Kenne can hear Steve asking the question.

"Yes, it was Santa Anita," Steve responds.

"Can you give me a description of this guy?"

"Hold on a minute," Steve says.

Kenne can hear some faint talking in the background that lasts almost a minute and then Steve comes back.

"He operates a ranch near here. He's about six-five, rugged looking and wears cowboy gear. You know, blue jeans, boots, wide-brimmed white cowboy hat. He was on his way to see a trainer by the name of Douglas Earlimart at the Santa Anita stables."

"What kind of vehicle was he driving?" Kenne asks.

Once again Steve leaves Kenne hanging as he talks to the lady.

"He's driving a 2012 blue Dodge Ram 1500 pickup, New Mexico plates B-I-G-D-R-N-C-H. It'll be pulling a horse trailer."

"Keep this to yourself," Kenne says. "I've got an unidentified dead man here that matches the description you gave me. Don't say anything to the lady there. I'll fax you a picture. See if she can identify him."

"I understand," Steve responds.

"What's her husband's name?"

"Dominic Treadway." Steve answers.

"Watch for the fax in the next few minutes and then call me."

Kenne hangs up his cell phone and sits back in his chair putting both hands up to his face and rubs it several times. A short time later he rises from his chair and picks up a picture for victim eighteen from his desk. He enters the squad room and faxes the picture to Steve whose number is in the machine's memory.

The squad members start arriving one at a time. When they are all there Kenne calls a meeting.

"For those who don't know, Domino struck again last night, twice," Kenne informs them.

They all shake their heads in amazement.

"It looks like instead of fleeing she's decided to put her activity into high gear. Victim number eighteen might be a rancher from New Mexico. I am waiting for confirmation on his identity. He was killed in a motel in Arcadia. Victim number nineteen is Timothy Bland, a twenty-six year old golf instructor. He was stabbed six times out in the open in Santa Monica. Lamar was with me when we investigated both scenes of the crimes. I believe he's finished with his reports on the two murders."

Lamar starts passing out the report along with pictures of the two victims. While he's doing that, Kenne's cell phone rings. He answers it in a rush. It's Steve Lockwood. He informs Kenne that Treadway's widow identified the faxed photo as her husband.

"That call was from New Mexico," Kenne states. "The photo I faxed to the

Highway Patrol in Santa Fe was identified by the victim's widow. His name is Dominic Treadway. He was driving a 2012 blue Dodge Ram 1500 pickup truck and it may be hauling a horse trailer. It has New Mexico personalized plates B-I-G-D-R-N-C-H. Big D Ranch. I believe Domino is now driving it as she abandoned her car earlier, yesterday."

"I'll get out an all-points on the truck," Sergeant Singleton volunteers.

****

Kenne takes Ramirez with him to interview horse trainer Earlimart regarding Treadway. Earlimart was shocked and saddened to hear about Treadway's fate. He informs Kenne that Treadway left his horse trailer in the parking lot behind the stables.

Earlimart said that Treadway first contacted him about a month ago in answer to an advertisement he placed in various newspapers in New Mexico regarding the sale of newborn foals. The foals were owned by financier Frederic Downing of The Downing Racing Foundation. Downing set up the foundation as a fund raiser for the upkeep and maintenance of retired race horses.

"He arrived a few days ago," Treadway continues his story. "We were negotiating price on two foals."

"Did he happen to give you any earnest money?" Kenne asks.

"No. We don't do business that way. But he did show me a wad of cash that he was ready to spend."

Before leaving Kenne and Ramirez inspect Treadway's trailer and find nothing helpful.

On the ride back to headquarters Kenne and Ramirez discuss what clue the two one sides domino implies.

"We've tried before with other numbers and have come up empty or on wild goose chases," Ramirez states.

"But we've been close and on the right track," Kenne proclaims. "We've got the numbers two and one. They total three. There has to be some correlation there."

"Two and one could also be twenty-one," Ramirez professes.

"For some reason I like the number three," Kenne says. "What if we set up a three-mile perimeter from the Santa Monica site?"

"Too small an area. Domino is smarter than that."

"Wait one second," Kenne says with a surprised look on his face. "Twenty-one. You said twenty-one. That's it. You're a genius."

"What's it?" Ramirez asks.

"The other night I wanted some company so I called Giana and we met at the Westwood Sports Lounge. While we were there, off and on, we were watching the Dodgers' game. After a bit Giana started acting kind of weird as if she had changed into Eliana in front of me. Anyhow, she made a comment about the Dodgers' pitcher that kind of stuck in my mind."

"What was the comment?" Ramirez asks.

"She said in a very nasty tone, 'That guys going to kill someone with that wild fastball. It's as if he's attacking the hitter'."

"Pitchers don't attack the hitter, they attack the strike zone," Ramirez profoundly declares.

"To continue. Right after that Giana got up and adjourned to the rest room without saying a word. When she came back she was her old self again. While she was gone I was watching the ball game. I remember that the Dodgers' pitcher wore number 21 but I don't remember his name."

"Number 21. That's Tommy Torrance," Ramirez says.

Both men look at each other in amazement. Kenne puts his siren and flashing lights on so they can hurry back to headquarters.

On the way, Kenne proclaims, "She's going to strike today. I can feel it in my bones. Maybe at two-ten."

"Maybe at three o'clock," Ramirez corrects him.

Chapter Twenty-Four

Gotcha!!!

Kenne Narration: "I've spent a lot of time the last few days educating myself about dissociative identity disorder. I think I've figured it out. At least I'm eighty-five percent positive. Here it is. Eliana is Domino and Giana has been protecting her because she knows about the Eliana personality. It was Giana's idea to befriend me so that she could protect herself with the information she was receiving from the bug on my jacket lapel. I am also pretty sure Eliana has no idea that Giana exists."

Immediately upon returning to headquarters Kenne contacts the Torrance Police Chief Erwin Leisner and the County Sheriff's District Office in San Pedro. He informs them that Domino may strike somewhere in Torrance. Chief Leisner offers his squad room for a briefing and Kenne accepts. Before heading out to Torrance, Kenne has Sam run one hundred copies of Giana's sketch and mug shot to be distributed to everyone at the briefing.

Kenne tells his squad, "We'll team up in pairs. Mac and Lamar, Dave and Bradley and Ramirez, you'll ride with me."

"Wait a minute," Sam's interrupts. "I've been cooped up in this office for too long. I want in on this."

Kenne looks at him, then at Trop, and says, "Sam, you team up with Trop. Let's move."

The squad heads down Interstate 405, the San Diego Freeway, to Torrance with sirens blaring and roof lights flashing. Kenne leads the way and the others follow close behind.

The Torrance Police Department's main headquarters is located on Civic Center Drive, not far from the freeway. There are six County Sheriff vehicles parked in front of the building when Kenne and his squad arrive. Chief Leisner and the Sheriff's Department San Pedro District Office Captain George Myers greet them. Leisner leads the way to the squad room where about one-hundred officers are assembled.

The drone of everyone talking is silenced when Leisner yells, "Let's get started. I want silence."

He introduces Kenne and turns the briefing session over to him. Kenne looks around the room before he gets started.

"Gentlemen and ladies, (Kenne nods his head and smiles at two female Torrance police officers sitting in the front row) I'm sure you are all familiar with the Domino case my squad has been working on. We are gathered here because we have confirmed information that Domino is a woman and she's going to strike again right here in Torrance, sometime this afternoon. Time is of the essence that we capture her.

"She is driving a blue 2012 Dodge Ram 1500 pickup truck with New Mexico personalized plates B-I-G-D-R-N-C-H. Big D Ranch. She probably doesn't know that we know she's in that vehicle. Do everything you can to take her alive. It's possible she may have stayed in a local motel or hotel overnight so we need to concentrate our efforts on the parking lots and ramps of those facilities in looking for the vehicle. Also shopping center parking lots might be another alternative because she may be looking to pick up her next victim with solicitation.

"She is probably armed with a knife or knives. I doubt that she has a fire arm but take precautions. She could be wearing a black-hooded sweat shirt. The hood might be raised over her head.

"Do not try and apprehend her alone if you spot her. Call for backup. If you find the truck and she is not in it, do not go near the truck. It may be wired to explode. Call for backup.

"There are sketch and mug shot copies of our suspect on the table behind me. Pick one up before leaving. The suspect could appear in either image. It is now one-forty. We think she may strike at either two-ten or three o'clock so let's hit the road. Everyone use channel nine to communicate."

Leisner instructs his officers to patrol their usual assigned area. He also suggests the county sheriff officers freelance as much as possible and patrol the motel and hotel parking areas as well as the shopping centers.

****

Kenne and Ramirez are cruising along Pacific Coast Highway for the past twenty minutes and no calls have come in. It's a little past two o'clock and Kenne is getting worried. Ramirez notices that he's on edge and suggests that he relax. Kenne agrees with him but gets on the radio.

"This is Lieutenant Quintcannon. Does anybody have anything to report? Please respond if you do."

Shortly after Kenne's transmission Lamar and Mac are sitting at a red light on Hawthorne Boulevard when a blue 2012 Dodge Ram 1500 pickup makes a right turn in front of them.

Mac points to the vehicle and says, "That might be what we're looking for?"

Lamar, who is driving, responds, "California plates."

"They could be stolen," Mac counters.

Lamar hits his siren and turns on the flashing lights and they take up the chase.

"Did you notice the driver?" Mac asks. "Could it have been a woman?"

"I didn't get a good look," Lamar answers.

After a short chase the vehicle pulls over. Lamar and Mac get out of their unmarked squad card with guns drawn and pointing.

"Raise your hands and stay in the vehicle," Lamar hollers instructions to the driver.

The driver, a woman does as Lamar instructs. Lamar and Mac move cautiously toward the vehicle. Lamar approaches the driver's side door at the same time Mac is at the passenger side.

"What in hell is this all about?" the woman yells.

"Don't make any sudden moves," Lamar continues with the instructions, "We need to see your driver's license and vehicle registration."

Moving slowly, the driver pulls her driver's license from her purse and the vehicle registration from the glove box. She hands them both to Lamar who examines them while keeping one eye on the driver.

"They match," he says. "She's okay."

"You still haven't told me what this is about," the woman says in a cruel tone.

"A stolen vehicle report," Mac says. "Similar to yours. I'll call in so you don't have any more trouble."

"Sorry ma'am," Lamar says. "You have a good day."

"Screw you," she responds.

****

2:10 comes and goes and nobody has reported any unusual action. About ten minutes later two uniform county sheriff officers are cruising through the Del Amo Shopping Center open parking area and they spot the pickup truck. They call it in.

"Don't go near it," Kenne transmits. "I've got a bomb squad standing by. I want the truck surrounded. All county sheriff deputies converge on the Del Amo Shopping Center open parking area. Form a one-hundred foot perimeter around the vehicle."

Kenne heads for the shopping center while Ramirez alerts the bomb squad. Mac reports they are close by and will be there in a couple minutes. It takes the bomb squad five minutes to arrive at the parking area. Kenne and Ramirez arrive shortly thereafter.

After a ten-minute search of the vehicle the bomb squad gives an all clear. Kenne and Ramirez search the vehicle and find a black-hooded sweat shirt on the front seat and a number of knives and clubs on the floor of the passenger side. They also find the remaining pieces of the domino set in a small plastic case on the floor next to the weapons. Kenne orders four sheriff deputies to stand guard at the pickup and then gives instructions to the remaining officers at the site.

"She's here," Kenne shouts. "Somewhere in the mall. Cover all exits. Mac, get on the radio and have all cars converge here. Then you and Lamar follow me and Ramirez. We're going to search the mall."

It only takes Mac about thirty-seconds to get the word out. She then runs to catch up with Kenne, Ramirez and Lamar. They enter the mall. Kenne and Ramirez go to the left. Mac and Lamar to the right. They are all wired for sound.

"Keep in touch," Kenne instructs.

Chief Leisner orders a number of his officers to join Kenne in searching the mall. Kenne's squad and the Torrance officers roam the mall for almost fifteen minutes with no results. Then one of the Torrance officers calls in that he thinks he has spotted Domino on the second floor of Macy's Department Store.

"Stay with her," Kenne instructs him. "We're on our way."

Domino sees the officer talking into his microphone on his collar and starts making her way toward a second floor exit that leads to a parking ramp.

The officer realizes what she is doing and calls in, "She's on the move."

Domino hurries her pace and then moves into a run after exiting toward the parking ramp. The officer follows, running as fast as he can while talking.

"She's on the run through the parking ramp. I'm following."

Officers in vehicles start converging toward the parking ramp.

Domino exits the parking ramp running at full speed and notices a young mother with a baby fastening the child into a car seat in a white, late model SUV. She runs up to the woman and grabs her from behind flashing a knife in her face.

"Get into the driver's seat and follow instructions," Domino says in a desperate tone of voice. "If you don't I'll kill the baby."

The baby's mother is trembling but manages to get in the driver's seat of the car. Domino gets into the back seat and sits down next to the baby. The officer sees what's happening and calls in the information that

Domino is hijacking a woman and her baby and gives a description of the vehicle.

Before domino can give the woman any instructions the vehicle is surrounded with Torrance and county sheriff police cars. Kenne and Ramirez arrive from their dash through the parking ramp. The non-driving police officers get out of their cars and start walking toward the SUV with guns drawn.

Kenne holds up his left arm and shouts, "Everybody, stop. Form a fifty-foot perimeter around the car."

As they obey Kenne, Domino orders the woman to start the engine. Still trembling from fear the woman does as she's told. Meanwhile, Kenne slowly approaches the SUV with arms extended showing no weapon. He asks the driver to lower the left rear window. She obliges and also lowers her window.

"It's over Giana," Kenne says. "I need you to step out of vehicle."

"Giana?" Domino questions. "Who the hell is Giana?"

Quickly, Kenne realizes that it's possible that Giana no longer exists in her mind.

"I'm sorry," Kenne recants. "I got a little confused. I meant to say Eliana."

Domino laughs and then in a sudden change of mood shouts, "Make room for us to drive away or I'll kill the baby."

"Now why would you want to do that?" Kenne asks. "We're here to help you stop doing things like that. We're here to help you, not hurt you."

"I won't say it again. Make room for us or I'll kill both of them."

Kenne looks Domino in the eyes and asks, "Don't you recognize me?"

Domino answers, "Why should I? I've never seen you before."

With that, Domino raises her arm with the knife and holds it over the baby's head.

"Don't do anything you'll regret later. Let's talk for awhile. It can't hurt to talk for awhile," Kenne tries coaxing her.

"I've got nothing to say to you. I don't know how you know about me and I don't care. Now, stop wasting everyone's time and let us pass."

"Please don't let her hurt my baby," the driver pleads

"Eliana, you know if you kill this lady and her baby you won't be able to leave any dominoes. What would your grandfather think of that?"

Domino is stunned by the remark.

"Leave him out of this," she snaps back.

Kenne shakes his head and says, "I'm afraid we can't."

"Why are you tormenting me?" Domino asks.

"Same question back at you, Eliana. Why are you tormenting us?"

"You don't understand."

"You're right. I don't understand. But I want to. We can start by you handing me the knife and stepping out of the vehicle."

Kenne moves a couple steps closer.

"Don't come any closer."

Kenne stops and continues, "I thought we had a deal here?"

"I haven't agreed to any deal." Domino shouts waving the knife in Kenne's direction.

"Where's Giana? Maybe I can talk to her."

"There you go with that Giana business, again. There's no Giana. I'm here alone."

"How about Ana or Priscilla? Are they there? Kenne asks.

"I hate that name. Go away. You're making my head pound."

"Which name do you hate, Ana or Priscilla?"

"Priscilla. I hate that name," she yells. "Go away. My head is pounding."

Domino rubs her forehead trying to make the pounding go away.

"I can stop the pounding if you give me the knife," Kenne says extending his arm.

"I can't do that."

"Sure you can. Turn the knife around and slowly hand it to me, handle first," Kenne instructs in a calm voice.

Domino stares at Kenne for about twenty seconds.

"If I give you the knife, what's going to happen to me?'

"Truthfully, in the long run I don't know. That's not up to me. But you'll be safe for now."

"Maybe I can trust you. I don't know. But I don't trust them."

She waves the knife at the police line surrounding the area.

"They're here for the same reason I am. They want to help you."

"That's why they've got their guns drawn? I don't think so."

"They've got their guns drawn because they're as confused as you and me at what's happening here."

"I want them to put their guns away," Domino insists.

Kenne shouts, "Holster your weapons," to accommodate Domino.

All officers follow the instructions. While they do so, Kenne looks around and notices three S.W.A.T. sharpshooters stationed on the second floor of the parking ramp. All three probably have a clear shot at

Domino through the rear window of the SUV.

"Things are getting rather serious and we don't have much time left so I'm going to ask you one more time to hand me the knife and step out of the vehicle," Kenne says in a warning overtone.

"I've decided I won't do that. It's time to let me pass or I will kill both of them."

"No you won't," Kenne says with authority.

"And who's going to stop me?"

"The three sharpshooters stationed on the second floor of the parking ramp behind you."

Domino turns her body around to get a look. She turns and looks at Kenne.

"You'd let them shoot me?"

"It's not up to me. You need to sit perfectly still. If you make a move toward either one of them, they have orders to shoot. Now will you give me the knife?"

Domino freezes but continues looking at Kenne.

"Promise you'll help me?" she pleads.

"I'll do what I can. But it's up to you. I'm going to need your help."

Domino reaches over cautiously and opens the door. She steps out of the vehicle and hands the knife, handle first, to Kenne. Ramirez, Mac and Lamar hustle over and handcuff her from behind. Kenne instructs Mac and Lamar to transport Domino to the lockup at headquarters.

Lamar leads Domino away toward a sheriff's patrol car and recites her rights.

The woman from the SUV runs up and hugs Kenne with tears in her eyes. She is so choked up that she cannot speak.

Mac looks at Kenne and says, "Thank God, it's over."

"Not yet," Kenne says.

Chapter Twenty-Five

Who is Priscilla?

Kenne Narration: "When I told Mac 'not yet' in rebuttal to her 'it's over' comment, I was dead serious. Sure, we had Domino, or Eliana, or Giana, or Priscilla … whichever identity she chooses to go by … in custody. The terror is over. The mystery is just beginning. It's time to question her. I want to understand what has been going on in her mind. I want answers to a thousand questions. No, I need answers to a thousand questions. I called Doctor Winslow and set up a time for her to meet with us"

Kenne, Captain Manning, Dr. Winslow and Deputy District Attorney Richard Neilsen are all standing and waiting in Kenne's office for Domino's court appointed Public Defender. The wait was about ten minutes when Rhoda Parsons strolls into Kenne's office. Kenne was not surprised that she had been appointed to the case.

Rhoda, who knows Ray Manning from the time she was being courted by Kenne, walks up and gives him a hug. He returns it.

She steps back and compliments him, "You look great. The fountain of youth."

"You're a vision of beauty yourself," he says returning the compliment.

Rhoda than walks over to Richard Neilsen and holds her hand out and they shake hands.

"Counselor, it's good to see you again," Neilsen says.

"You too. I'm looking forward to an exciting court battle, if it comes to that."

"You two know each other?" Kenne asks.

"We've had a few legal battles," Neilsen says.

Rhoda then turns her attention toward Dr. Winslow and greets her, "You must be Doctor Patricia Winslow."

"Yes, I am," Dr. Winslow confirms and holds out her hand to shake.

Rhoda ignores the gesture and pulls up a chair in front of Kenne's desk.

"My first order of business is when are you going to release Jason Poe?" Rhoda asks looking at Kenne.

"When we are one-hundred percent positive he hasn't been an accomplice in the serial killings," Kenne firmly answers.

Rhoda looks at Kenne with an evil glare in her eyes and then continues.

"I just came from a two hour session with my client, Eliana. She is a very sick woman. I've got her waiting for us in your interrogation room one but before we get started with our session I want to lay out some ground rules," Rhoda states.

"There are no ground rules," Captain Manning informs her.

"There is today or we call this off."

"What did you have in mind?" Kenne asks.

"Number one, there will be no taping of the session. That's voice and video. Number two, only one of you will ask the questions and it won't be Dr. Winslow. She's just an observer today. I don't want Eliana confused with medical mumbo jumbo."

"I understand," Dr. Winslow says nodding her head.

"I'll be handling the questions," Kenne says.

"Number three. Her name is Eliana. If you call her by any other name it will confuse her. Number four. If she doesn't answer any questions, don't try to pry an answer from her. It will probably upset her."

"That's it?" Kenne asks.

"That's it," Rhoda answers.

"Fair enough," Kenne agrees. "Let's adjourn to number one."

****

Eliana is sitting with her head down staring at her handcuffed hands at the table in interrogation room one when everyone enters. She continues to sit motionless and doesn't even lift her head to see who is joining her as everyone sits down at the table.

Rhoda sits down next to Eliana to her left while Captain Manning sits at the end of the table near Eliana. Dr. Winslow sits at the opposite end near Rhoda. Kenne sits down opposite Eliana and opens his note pad. Deputy D.A. Neilsen takes a seat next to him.

"Eliana, look at me," Rhoda instructs her client.

Eliana lifts her head slowly and looks at Rhoda.

"Let me introduce you to everybody. The lady on my left is Dr. Patricia Winslow. She is a dissociative identity disorder expert. Do you remember we talked about that?"

"Yes," Eliana says nodding her head.

"The gentleman sitting across from me is Richard Neilsen. He's a deputy district attorney representing Los Angeles County. The man sitting across the table from you is Lieutenant Kenne Quintcannon and the man next to you is Captain Ray Manning. Both of them are with the Los Angeles County Sheriff's Department. Lieutenant Quint-cannon has some questions he's going to ask you. If you feel that your rights as I informed you about earlier are being violated, you don't have to answer those questions. Do you understand?"

"Yes, I understand?" Eliana answers.

Rhoda nods at Kenne and says, "Go ahead but be careful."

"Hi, Eliana," Kenne greets her.

"Hi," she says nodding her head.

"Do you remember me from yesterday?"

"I do."

"Do you believe that I'm trying to help you? In other words, do you trust me?"

"I trust Rhoda," Eliana answers. "I'm still trying to figure out if I believe you. Why are all these other people here?"

"Whether you believe it or not they are here because they also want to help you with your problem."

Eliana looks at Rhoda and asks, "Do you believe they want to help me?"

"I believe they want to help you in different ways," Rhoda answers.

Eliana slowly turns her head toward Kenne and asks, "Do you know about the agony I've been going through?"

"Why don't you tell us about it? You'll feel a lot better."

Eliana glances at Rhoda who nods her head that it's okay.

"I … I … I … I'm confused about a lot of it. There were times I can't remember.

Like I was … I was unconscious. You know, not aware of what was going on around me."

"Take your time," Kenne says passionately. "Why don't you start with the dominoes?"

She looks at Kenne with terror on her face and then it soon turns to a smile and she laughs.

"That's a good place as any because it all started with that."

"Your grandpa?" Kenne asks.

"How do you know about him?"

"You left a trail and we picked it up."

"But I was so careful."

"Why did you leave the dominoes as clues?"

"Just like grandpa. I was playing a game with you."

"How did you find out about Albert Hill," Kenne asks.

"From grandma. I went to live with her when I was twelve, maybe thirteen."

"Why did you go to live with your grandma?"

"My mom got sick and went away."

"How about your dad?"

"He was always in trouble. I think he was in jail."

"Just what did your grandma tell you about grandpa?"

"One day I asked her about him. You know, where was he at? Why wasn't he living with her? She told me the whole story about him. Why they never got married."

"And why didn't they get married?" Kenne asks.

"It was because he wanted to protect her she said. You know, protect her from what he was doing?"

"Can you tell me about that time of your life?"

"It's kind of hazy. I don't remember a lot."

"Tell me what you do remember?"

Eliana closes her eyes and after about ten seconds starts to twitch. Shortly after that her whole body shakes. Kenne reaches out and sets his right hand on her left hand. After a bit Eliana stops shaking and opens her eyes.

"Are you okay?" Kenne asks.

Eliana looks at Kenne and tears start to form in her eyes.

"The bastards," she cries out. "They shouldn't have done that to me."

She moves her handcuffed hands away from Kenne's hand and wipes the tears from her face. More flow and Captian Manning hands her his handkerchief. She takes it and wipes the rest of the tears from her eyes and face.

"Thank you," she says in a soft voice.

She holds onto the handkerchief with her right hand.

"If you don't want to talk about that we can move on to something else," Kenne says attempting to comfort her.

"No. It's okay. I need to talk about it. I need to get it out."

"Are you sure?" Rhoda asks.

Eliana nods her head several times.

"Take your time," Kenne suggests.

"I … I was fourteen. There were three of them. They raped me over and over and over and over until I couldn't feel anything anymore."

She pauses and takes a deep breath.

"Who were they?" Kenne asks.

"From my high school."

"Did you report it to the police?"

"No. I told grandma and she told me not to. She knew what I was going through and it would just be harder on me to go through it again by talking about it."

"And then what?" Kenne asks.

"I tried to forget what happened. Sometimes I was able to do that. But then it would come back again and again. Then I … I … I decided to pay them back for what they did."

"And what was that?"

Eliana looks Kenne in the eye and smiles.

"I killed all three of them," she says without showing any emotion.

Everybody in the room look at each other with their eyes open wide.

"Do you want to tell me about it?" Kenne asks.

"How much trouble will I be in if I do?" She answers with a question of her own.

"I don't know. It's not up to me."

"Is it up to him?" she asks pointing at Deputy D.A. Neilsen.

"Actually, I have the feeling it will be in the hands of doctors and a judge. Do you understand that?"

Eliana nods her head and says, "I understand."

She stares into Kenne's eyes for a moment and he returns the stare.

"They violated me. They had to die. The first one was easy. It was winter time and he was chopping firewood. He laid the ax down to get more wood and I picked it up, snuck up behind him and drove it into his back. I had gloves on so no finger prints were on the ax handle."

"Do you remember how you felt afterwards?"

"Yeah. One down and two to go."

Kenne looks at Rhoda for a moment. She returns the glance and shrugs her shoulders.

"Tell me about the other two," Kenne says.

"Do we really have to do this?" Rhoda asks.

"I don't know. Why don't you ask Eliana?" Kenne answers.

"No. I need to," Eliana says. "I've been carrying this around too long."

"Okay," Rhoda says with a nod of her head.

Eliana returns her attention toward Kenne.

"The other two weren't so easy. They were scared about what happened to their pal. Whenever they'd see me they would give me an evil eye but they never said anything to anybody.

"One of them used to drive an old pickup truck. One day I spotted the truck at the far end of the school parking lot. I walked over and looked into the driver's side window. There he was on top of some girl going at it. I saw a tire iron lying on the bed of the pickup. I grabbed it, opened the door of the truck and stabbed him many times. The girl screamed so I had to kill her too.

"You understand, don't you? I couldn't leave a witness."

"I understand," Kenne says. "Then what did you do?"

"I knew as soon as the third one found out about what I did he would surely go to the police and tell them about me and why I was doing this. I knew where he lived so I took the tire iron with me and went to his house. The back door was unlocked and I entered the house. He was alone, sitting in the parlor watching television. I snuck up behind him and hit him in the head with the tire iron. There was blood everywhere. I just kept hitting him and hitting him."

"That's enough," Rhoda cries out.

Kenne holds up his right hand as if to tell Rhoda he's not through.

"Do you want to take a break?" Kenne asks Eliana.

"No. I'm fine. Really."

"Did you feel better after that?" Kenne asks.

"I don't know. I guess so. I don't remember much. Things started going in and out after that. You know, hazy. Most of the time I was okay. But I really don't remember a lot."

"Did you know that the Atlanta Police Department was looking for you in connection with the death of your two husbands?"

"They were Ana's husbands, not mine."

"Ana Trout?" Kenne says in a puzzled voice as he looks around at everyone in the room.

"You know about her?"

"Not everything. Why don't you tell us about her?"

Eliana takes a deep breath and sighs.

"Ana was my best friend in high school. We palled around together after that awful thing happened to me. We drifted apart after high school. Years later someone told me where she was and I went to visit her. We became friends again. When they did bad things to her I had to make them pay for it."

"Like those boys?"

"Yeah, like those boys. I had to kill them."

"Whatever happened to Ana?"

"She's dead."

"How did she die?"

"I don't know. She got sick, I guess."

"I want you to think about this question very carefully before you answer it? Okay?"

"Okay," Giana answers.

"Did Ana Trout die before or after you killed her husbands?"

Everybody in the room look at each other with very puzzled looks on their face. Eliana stares at Kenne for close to thirty seconds and finally answers the question.

"I don't understand. That's a confusing question."

"Never mind. It's not important right now. Let's move on. Do you know a man named Jason Poe?"

A mean look appears on Eliana's face and she doesn't answer the question.

"Did you hear my question, Eliana?" Kenne asks.

"I heard you," Eliana shouts.

Kenne doesn't say anything waiting for an answer.

Finally, Eliana answers in a calm voice, "I know him."

"What do you think of him?"

"He's an asshole. I hate him."

"Do you hate him because he made you become a serial killer?"

"I hate him because he abused me."

"You mean that domestic violence thing?"

"Yeah."

"Then he had nothing to do with your rampage?"

"Not exactly," she states.

"What do you mean by that?" Kenne asks with a puzzled look on his face.

"I decided he needed to be mentally tortured like I've been so I created the domino scheme to frame him as a serial killer. It almost worked."

"Once again, why did you leave the dominoes as clues?"

"The voices told me to do it."

"Your grandpa's voice?" Kenne asks startling Eliana.

She gives him a demonic stare before answering.

"He told me to finish what he started."

"Did he tell you once or more than once?" Kenne asks as if to humor her.

"He kept telling me over and over. I had to listen to him. He was my grandpa. You understand, don't you?"

Rhoda interrupts and says, "I think that's enough."

Kenne looks toward Rhoda and then Dr. Winslow. Dr. Winslow nods her head in agreement.

"Let's take a break," Kenne says. "We'll meet back here in twenty minutes."

****

Rhoda, Deputy D. A. Neilsen and Dr. Winslow use the time to return phone messages. Kenne returns Eliana to the lockup and then he and Captain Manning each grab a cup of coffee and adjourn to the Captain's office.

They sit in the office for more than five minutes without saying a word until Manning starts a conversation.

"That's the most depressing interrogation I've ever been part of," Manning states.

"That woman has had more things going on in her head than arguments in Congress." Kenne says.

"She's so mentally unstable that I don't think we can get a murder conviction," Manning predicts. "You know Rhoda is going to plead insanity."

"I agree. Let's see what Neilsen has to say when we get back in there."

"What do you want to do with Poe?"

"Let's hold him until we get a psychiatric evaluation on Eliana."

"That's what I was thinking."

Kenne looks at his watch and tells Manning, "Our twenty minutes are up. Let's get back in there."

****

Kenne and Manning are the first ones to return to interrogation room one. They take their original seats. The others file in one at a time about thirty-seconds apart and also take their original seats.

"Where's my client?" Rhoda asks.

"I thought it would be better if we finish this up without her," Kenne answers.

Rhoda stares at Kenne and asks, "Just what have you got going on in that criminologist mind of yours?"

Kenne holds up his left hand as a signal for Rhoda to wait for his answer. He then turns his attention toward Deputy D. A. Neilsen.

"Richard, can you give me your perspective on the session we had with Eliana?"

Richard snickers and shakes his head before answering.

"I don't think we would get past a preliminary hearing without a judge declaring her mentally unstable to stand trial. I also assume my opposing counsel will file for psychiatric evaluations and after the results are in plead not guilty by reason of insanity."

Richard looks at Rhoda and raises his eyebrows.

"You've read my mind, Counselor," Rhoda says with a wide grin.

"Speaking of psychiatric evaluation," Kenne remarks. "What have you got to say about our serial killer, Dr. Winslow?"

"Right now, I really can't give you an opinion without examining her in private which would include hypnosis. Of course, I would need her consent and probably yours also, Counselor."

"How long would that take?" Rhoda asks. "An hour, two hours?"

"It's not that simple. I can't give you a time frame. It might take two hours and then again it might take several days."

"I'll discuss it with her as soon as we're finished here."

"I don't have anything else," Kenne says.

Deputy D. A. Neilsen rises from his chair and states, "Keep me informed when Dr. Winslow has finished her evaluation so I can schedule a preliminary hearing."

He leaves the room just as everybody else rises from their chairs.

"Lieutenant, may I see you for a moment in private?" Dr. Winslow asks Kenne.

"Sure," Kenne responds.

Rhoda and Captain Manning leave the room, closing the door behind them. Kenne is much taller than Dr. Winslow so he sits down on the corner of the table so the doctor doesn't have to look up at him.

"What's on your mind?" Kenne asks.

"I want to commend you for the way you handled that interrogation. It really showed compassion."

"Thank you."

"If I'm going to do psychological therapy on Eliana I need her transferred to the Psych Ward at L. A. General."

"No problem but it will have to be in maximum security."

"That'll be fine."

"Just a bit of heads up for you, doctor. FBI Agent Parker Cunningham has been involved in this case of late. He had the IRS run a profile on Ana Trout's past employment history. He emailed the information to me last night. It seems Eliana as Ana Trout has done a lot of moving around. There are employment information documents from Memphis, Kansas City, Dallas and Phoenix before she settled here. Cunningham has all of those local FBI offices checking on unsolved murders during the time she worked in those cities."

"Thank you for that information. And what's up with that question about Eliana killing Ana Trout before or after she killed her husbands?"

"I have a theory which you probably could confirm under hypnosis."

"And your theory is?" Dr. Winslow asks.

"Eliana … or should I say Priscilla was so enamored with Ana while they were friends that she actually wanted to be Ana. So she killed Ana and took over her identity including her personality."

"What about Priscilla's two marriages?"

"That's the easy part. Her grandmother planned her weddings so she married her two husbands under her real name, Priscilla. But when it came time to kill them, she was doing it for Ana. It's just a theory."

"Lieutenant, you have a vivid imagination."

"Sometimes it gets me in trouble."

****

Kenne Narration: "My imagination was about to get me in trouble. In trouble with my bank account. I was imagining a two-week stay at the beach in Waikiki with Alicia. I called and asked her if she'd be interested and she said yes, yes, yes, but needed to ask for vacation time at work.

Eliana was reluctant to go into hypnosis therapy with Dr. Winslow but when Rhoda said it was the only way she could properly defend her she agreed. A little more than two weeks had passed when I finally got a call from Dr. Winslow that she wanted to meet with me, Rhoda, Deputy D. A. Neilsen and FBI Agent Cunningham at her office. I made calls to everybody."

Kenne and Agent Cunningham were the first to arrive at Doctor Winslow's office at the Clinic for Dissociative Identity Disorders. Deputy D. A. Neilsen and Rhoda arrived within minutes. Doctor Winslow greets them all and introduces herself to Agent Cunningham. Winslow's four guests are asked to have a seat on two couches at both sides of the room. Doctor Winslow sits down on the front edge of her desk.

"You all know why we're here so let's get started," Winslow says. "I've talked with Priscilla for six hours … and we'll call her Priscilla because that's her birth name … and given her twenty-two hours of hypnosis sessions. I can use the words psychopath, sociopath, psychotic and the like to describe Priscilla. Or all of the above wrapped into one. But we'll refrain from that right now. I won't bore you with twenty-two hours of the hypnosis therapy, just the highlights. My God, what highlights. If anyone has questions, please ask them as we go.

"Contrary to everyone's thinking Priscilla's problem didn't start with those three boys raping her. It goes back much further than that. You have to understand that she was born into a dysfunctional family. Her grandfather, Albert Hill was a serial killer. Her mother was mentally unstable and her father was an abusive criminal. She was abused as a child and she inherited all her family's dysfunctions. Things started to change for the good when she moved in with her grandmother. Then the rape.

"Soon after that event her brain created another personality named Eve to protect her from the conscious memory of the rape."

"She chose the name Eve from the movie 'The Three Faces of Eve'," Kenne states positively.

"Exactly," Winslow answers. "It seems that movie left a lasting impression on her when she first saw it as a child. Priscilla's brain turned her into Eve as she created a whole new personality. However, whenever she would see any of the rapists, the Priscilla part of her brain would take over. That's why she killed them, so she could live in peace as Eve. No remembrances.

"But Eve became a bore to her. She became so enamored of her friend Ana Trout that she wanted to be like her. Instead of being like her, she killed her and became Ana Trout. So Lieutenant, that question you asked Priscilla if she killed Ana before her husbands was right on but it really confused Priscilla. She didn't know how you found out about that. That's why she took so long to answer and got the answer you did.

"You were also right about the two marriages under her birth name. However, she lived those marriages as Ana Trout. When the husbands abused her it woke up the anger in Priscilla and she killed them both."

"Where did she bury them?" Agent Cunningham asks.

"The first husband was a stone mason. He kept cement blocks in storage in back of the house. She killed him with one of his tools and tied cement blocks to his arms and legs and dumped the body in a lake. She watched it sink."

"How was she able to handle the dead weight of the body and cement blocks?" Kenne asks.

"Although she has a small frame and doesn't have much strength as Ana or her other alter egos, Priscilla, when in a rage her will was very strong and she could do things that were not normal."

"You said alter egos," Kenne says. "Were there more than two?"

"We're getting to that."

Everybody in the room look at each other with puzzling looks.

"Priscilla's second husband died of rat poisoning. She buried his body next to their house and created a rose garden over his grave. When the police came around asking questions about his disappearance she knew it was time to leave. Using Ana's identification she left the Atlanta area and headed west. She stopped in Memphis, Tennessee and got work there. She remained in Memphis for about nine months and lived a normal life as Ana.

"Then one day, without provocation, Priscilla appeared in her brain. She was upset because she didn't like Memphis or some of the people at Ana's workplace. She was especially upset at the manager of Ana's shift. The lady befriended her and Priscilla didn't like the attention at first. Then she realized Ana needed some sort of companionship to show that she was a normal person. That is if you can call an added mental identity normal."

"So Priscilla killed her, right," Kenne states.

"She not only killed the lady but also took her identity and identification items, driver's license, credit cards and the like along with them upon leaving Memphis the next day. She settled in the Kansas City, Missouri area a few days later and obtained a job under Ana's persona as a hospital orderly. Actually, Priscilla, Ana and her added identity, Elizabeth obtained the job."

"So she now had three identities?" Rhoda asks.

"Yes. But there's more. Because of the three identities or alter egos, Priscilla's life was a mess. She had trouble adjusting to her surroundings because there was conflict between the Ana and Elizabeth personalities. So, Priscilla had to find a way of getting rid of the Elizabeth identity."

"She couldn't kill her. She was already dead," Rhoda says.

"Priscilla killed the identity, not the person," Winslow informs the group.

"How in the world did she do that?" Deputy D. A. Neilsen asks.

"Simple. She had the Elizabeth part of her brain kill a fellow worker and leave a handbag with her identification next to the body. In Priscilla's mind she knew the police would be looking for Elizabeth so she erased her memory.

"She also killed one other person in Kansas City but couldn't remember the details."

Doctor Winslow looks at her watch and informs everyone, "I've got another appointment in twenty minutes, so I'll make the rest of this short. After Kansas City, Priscilla moved to Dallas, Texas where she killed one person and then on to Phoenix, Arizona where there were two more victims. In every case, she assumed the identity of the person she killed to keep Ana from being lonely and used the same M. O. when she committed the murders. After that she settled here and of course the rest you know.

"If you want complete details of my sessions with Priscilla, I have video discs I can furnish you. But beware, they're very graphic."

"What do you recommend at this point, doctor?" Rhoda asks. "I mean, can she be treated for this disease."

"It's not a disease. It's a mental disorder. In answer to your question can she be treated the answer is yes. With medication, counseling and therapy. A lot of therapy. In answer to your question what do I recommend my answer is we need a judge to make that determination."

"What is your opinion on her standing trial for all those murders?" Neilsen asks.

Winslow snickers and says, "My opinion. It would be a waste of time, effort and the taxpayer's money."

"Can she be cured?" Neilsen continues with the questions.

"Who knows? If so, it could take years. But curing her would probably only relieve her of the conflict within her brain. She wouldn't be fit for society. But then that's my opinion."

Winslow glances at her watch and announces, "We're through. My next appointment will be here soon."

Everybody rises and heads for the door.

"I'm going to want a copy of those discs," Cunningham informs Winslow.

"I'll see that you get them by the end of the day," Winslow says. "Oh, Lieutenant can I see you for a moment?"

Kenne nods his head. Everyone else leaves the room. Winslow rises from her perch on the desk.

"I hope you're satisfied with my findings?" Winslow says.

"I can live with it."

"Now, do I bill the county for my time, or what?"

"One of the serial killing victims was a cousin of the actor Tony Deerfield and he offered a reward for the capture and conviction of the person that killed his cousin."

"Yes, I remember that," Winslow says.

"Well, I gave his agent a call and we had a long conversation regarding that reward."

Kenne reaches into his inside jacket pocket and pulls out a sealed envelope. He hands it to Winslow.

"He delivered this to me this morning. Open it."

Winslow opens the envelope and pulls out a check. She reads the amount of $100,000 and it's made out to her clinic. A large smile lights up her face.

"I hope that'll cover your expenses. Consider it a donation from Mr. Deerfield," Kenne says with a grin.

"It'll do," Winslow says as she gives Kenne a kiss on the cheek.

****

Kenne Narration: "Instead of returning Priscilla to our lockup, I had Captain Manning authorize her stay at the Maximum Security Psych Ward at L. A. General. Deputy D. A. Neilsen scheduled a preliminary hearing and Rhoda called in two psychiatrists to examine Priscilla. At the preliminary hearing Doctor Winslow and the two psychiatrists all testified that Priscilla was not mentally competent to stand trial even though she knew that her actions were unlawful. Neilsen & Rhoda could not reach a plea agreement and left the final decision in the hands of the presiding judge.

After due deliberation, the judge stated at Priscilla's sentencing that 'There is no agreement between the mental health and legal fields that a person can be acquitted due to a dissociative identity disorder diagnosis. The crimes the defendant has committed are truly heinous against society. Because medical testimony at the preliminary hearing is consistent that the defendant is not mentally competent to stand trial I am forced to sentence her to confinement in the Maximum Security section of L. A. General Hospital's Psych Ward until which time she can be cured of her mental disorder. When and if she is cured she shall stand trial for her crimes against society.

The judge also assigned Doctor Winslow to continue examination and therapy on Priscilla and report to the court on her progress. And me. I was relieved it was finally over and looking forward to my next assignment. But first I followed up on that great imagination of mine. I took a two week vacation in Hawaii. Yes, Alicia came with me."